FROM NOVEMBER ON

Cover art by Rii Finley:
iStock Photo 2161008187 Licensed.
Internal illustrations by Rii Finley:
iStock Photo 1003332724 Licensed

ISBN:
979-8-9995821-2-6 (Paperback)
Riifinley.com

1st edition 2026

Content Warnings:

Alright, so, here's the deal. This book is obviously set in a pretty harsh world; that being said, it may not be for all readers. I also include some sensitive topics and things certain people might consider taboo. Some of these warnings are soft spoilers, so do with that what you will.

This is an MMFM Why Choose with open door, explicit sex scenes, including MM.

Other potentially triggering topics include:
Forced Marriage
Patriarchal Tyranny
Brainwashing
Cult Behavior
Panic and Anxiety Attacks
Mentions of Abuse and Scars
Execution of an Allegedly Pregnant Woman
On-Page Murder(s) including Knife Violence
Sex in a Public Place
Siblings "Parking in the Same Garage" aka DVP

If you've ever screamed "Fuck the patriarchy!" while also wanting to get railed by three men... Buckle up.

White. Such an unfamiliar color—at least for *my* wardrobe. The symbol of purity, though a troubling number of women play a dangerous game and give theirs up before this day. Weddings used to be sacred, a beautiful union built on the foundations of love and devotion, according to our limited supply of history books. I know very little of the world that used to be, the one we failed. Maybe it was never truly meant for us.

Who awaits me on the other side of the embellished altar room doors is a mystery. Women never know who they will be bound to until these doors open. I'll do my best to be a worthy wife, and part of me hopes that, since I've been a self-respecting woman and maintained my innocence, The Powers Above will be gracious and place me with one of our kinder men.

Despite a lifetime of marital training—classes in obedience, life skills, and men's needs, driving home the rules of New Promise—in preparation to be the perfect wife, I can't shake the tightness in my chest or the irregular thumping of my pulse. I swallow hard, as if pebbles line my throat. There's no turning back, not that I could if I wanted.

This is my duty, my sole purpose in life, as The Powers Above demand.

Weddings, as we know them now, are nothing more than a man staking his claim on the woman of his choosing, and someone has actually chosen me. Best not to keep him waiting.

Three, two... I inhale, attempting to calm my trembling bones.

Anyone is better than dying by Raymond's hand.

One.

A faint nod to the guard on my left, and the doors swing open.

Our whole community is here, filling this marble chapel to the brim, as with every marital bonding. Columns are lined with opulent tapestries, and the floor has been polished to perfection. Everything is as it should be to please The Powers Above.

Practiced and prepared, my feet move on muscle memory alone, guiding me forward in a ritualistic half-step march. Faces of people I may never see again blur when my attention zeros in on the man standing at the end of the aisle.

Tall, with lean muscles shrouded by his white tunic. Slicked-back hair, almost unnaturally black, frames his angular face. Deep brown eyes track my every step—gentle, yet intense. With his notably darker skin tone and calm, yet powerful energy, he's an unmistakable member of the remnants of humanity.

Leo Koeler; the community enigma. His happenings are unknown to most. As a historian, he's a member of the select few entrusted with the care of ancient artifacts. What that truly means is privileged information. The weight of his position in the community settles in my bones like solid stone.

I'm about to marry one of the most prestigious men in New Promise.

Historians are notorious for their personalities —or lack thereof—usually described as reclusive and self-righteous. Leo, at the very least, fits the definition of the former. I had hoped for a husband who would show interest in social events so that I might maintain my acquaintanceships with the other women in my group. We may not be permitted to speak without our husbands' consent, but a few of them are married to kinder men.

Seeing the community hermit awaiting me at the altar squashes that foolish daydream.

My only real knowledge of Leo is that he's five years my senior and hardly ever attends non-mandated functions. There have been speculations that he would never choose a bride; at this moment, I wish it was not me.

Approaching the end of the aisle, a young guard with hair the color of embers stands next to Prime Guide Ogden. I've never seen him before, but his focus is solely on me. With the addition of his attention, the world feels too heavy. My body trembles as reality strikes harder than Raymond ever could.

In the same breath, my knees weaken completely, failing to support me. Clumsily, I stumble and nearly collapse, but Leo is quick to spare me the utter embarrassment. With uncanny speed, he gathers me in his, admittedly warm and welcoming, arms and rights me.

"Do be careful, Darling," he mutters in a hushed tone, meant for my ears alone, then leans away.

As Prime Guide Ogden begins his announcement, Leo's eyes are unmoving, intently focused on my being.

"Historian marriages are some of the most sacred in New Promise. I am pleased you've finally decided on a wife, Leo." Directing his full attention to my soon-to-be husband, Prime Guide continues, "While the Guides may not entirely agree with your... choice—" He flicks his cold gaze to me for a moment. "—they must honor it. Miss Harding has done well in her training and will undoubtedly be a dutiful and non-disruptive woman. What she lacks in pedigree, she makes up for in beauty and etiquette. Therefore, if you are pleased with your decision, despite her slight mishap, we will move forward."

"Prime Guide," Leo starts, tone sharper than a moment ago, as he turns and addresses the scrawny old man between us. "Pardon my brashness, but I'll have all of New Promise know that the future Mrs. Koeler will *not* be labeled as merely *adequate* due to her appearance and passive nature. My wife will command the same respect I'm given."

The conviction in his voice sends unfamiliar feelings coursing through my body—tingling in my toes, a lightness in my chest. The societal pressure and weight of their expectations feel somehow lessened by his simple proclamation. I'm uncertain what to make of it.

While he states one thing, I know the stories that circulate in New Promise. Men often present as saviors, or loving, charitable husbands at the altar, and then—sometimes only hours later—their truth comes to light.

Men do not care about women.

There's no chance that I, of all people, have found the one that does.

This is simply another "wedding", an old word taken on a new meaning. I'm property, and after he claims me before The Powers Above, the whole community will know I'm *his*.

"I did not intend to speak of her in a negative manner. I merely aimed to inform you that, while the future *Mrs. Koeler* may not have been born into a family as esteemed as your own, she will make a suitable wife. Surely, the son she gives you will be well looked after. So, without further interruption, let us commence with the ceremonial bonding."

With the red-haired guard on our heels, Prime Guide Ogden leads us to the back chamber of the chapel. More marble walls greet us, only these are lined with tapestries decorated with ancient symbols and crests from lost human civilizations. Nobody is entirely sure how long ago these "countries" existed, but their banners are fascinating. I find the symbol for the one called "Canada" the most endearing. It is nothing more than a vibrant red leaf. The tree species it belonged to is long gone, likely another victim of the collapse. Perhaps the tragedy makes it beautiful.

"Phoebe," Leo utters my name as if he's practiced it, holding his hand out to me. I stare into his nearly black gaze. "I'm sorry. This will be the only time I inflict pain or do any harm to you, without your explicit permission."

Right, I had almost forgotten why we are here.

Nodding, I place my hand in his, palm-side up. My skin tingles where it lies against his warmth. With a faint squeeze, the injection needle quickly slips the small implant, filled with poison, under my skin. As I wince, he chews his full lower lip, brows pulled tightly together.

I can't hear the words Prime Guide Ogden is chanting beside us. A lifetime of training could never effectively prepare you for *this*. There is merely a brief mention in all our courses. Everyone knows a husband holds the key to his wife's life; one wrong move and it could all be over at his will. It's terrifying, which I suppose is why the topic is so taboo.

"I know my duties and will ensure you never need to use this, Master." Avoiding his eyes, I offer a slight bow. To my left, the mysterious guard swallows hard, audibly so. I catch the faintest twitch of his hand, but do not allow myself to linger and return my focus to our ceremony.

Warm fingers trail along my jaw, cupping gently to lift my head. "You'll never call me 'Master' again after this. You may call me Leo until you're comfortable with 'Husband' or whichever term you prefer. Understood?" A calm command, not born of anger, but of some other emotion I'm not familiar with.

Breath stuttering, I supply a shaky nod in response.

The young guard catches my eye once more, curiosity in his expression giving me pause. It's as if he's admiring how kindly Leo treats me. I can't allow myself to keep getting distracted by him, as it would surely mean my death. This must be a test of my resolve.

Prime Guide Ogden strikes a match, and before long, smoke from our ceremonial incense fills the air. Our marital chamber comes alive with the scents of vanilla and cinnamon. He completes his incantation and blesses us both in the name of The Powers Above before leaving with his guard.

Just like that, I'm a wife... to the mysterious Leo Koeler, no less.

Surely, a traditional wedding was much more eventful and meaningful than this savagery.

As the lock on our chamber door engages, we're left alone to complete our ceremony. A large bed lies against the far wall, made with stark white sheets. No matter how many times I told myself I'd be ready for this, I'm not. My breathing speeds up to an uncontrollable pace, and I nearly crumble under the weight of our impending consummation.

Eyes darting around the room, a sweat breaks out along my brow as I work to take in air. Shaking away my reservations, I silently reassure myself that I can manage this. Failing now is not an option, I must stand strong and accept my new life.

I'll have to service him as he pleases from this moment forth.

They say the first time is the worst; may as well get it over with.

I begin fumbling with the ties on my marital tunic. My trembling hands fail to grasp the thin cords, and I curse the Guides under my breath.

"Phoebe, relax for me. I have no intention to copulate with you, not like this." Leo's large hands land on my shoulders, snapping the tightly wound thread that has been wrapping itself around my psyche. Gently, he slides them up to frame my face.

"You... don't?" I manage to swallow a sob just as it attempts to escape. "Are you unhappy with your choice?" Wavering, I hold my breath awaiting his reply. The previously heavy air thins, and I feel as though I might faint.

Keep it together, fainting isn't real.

Fortunately, he's a benevolent man and doesn't leave me wondering.

"Darling." Sighing, he brushes his thumbs across my cheeks. I close my eyes for a moment, finding the sensation quite calming. "We will eventually, but only when you're ready. I intend to be patient and earn it."

I startle as he leans in and presses his lips to my forehead with a tenderness I've never witnessed from a man. Darkness of some sort flashes in his eyes as he pulls back.

I curl my lips between my teeth, chin trembling.

The flare of Leo's nostrils nearly breaks me, an all-too-familiar precursor to rage. "They're true, aren't they, the stories about your father? You don't have to say anything if it's too difficult. Just nod if I'm right. He hurts you, doesn't he?"

Golden-painted etchings on the bedposts behind him serve as a focal point while I pull my thoughts together. I'm not sure why he's asking. Maybe this is part of his manipulation tactics? It could be entertaining for him, seeing how long he can convince me that he's different. Surely his motives are self-serving.

But what if it's not an act? Dare I believe I'm the fortunate one?

We stand in silence for some time, neither of us moving. A faint breeze drifts through the nearly empty room from the lone open window. The incense lit for our ceremony fully extinguishes, and the last of its sweet, spicy scent fades.

Eventually, my bare feet ache from standing on the solid floor, begging for relief. Tiring from my adrenaline waning, I let my eyes meet his. Shoulders dropping, I give in and nod, almost indiscernible.

He closes his eyes and pulls a deep breath through his nose as he steps away.

I watch his chestnut-colored knuckles fade to white as his hands tighten into fists. Through the thin fabric of his marital tunic, the tension in his broad shoulders is glaringly obvious.

Curling into myself, I link my hands together and drop to my knees. "P-please forgive me for upsetting you. If you must use me to release your emotions, may I ask only that you do not harm m-my face? Those are always the hardest bruises to conceal."

Expression softening, he moves slowly and kneels at my side. I tremble harder in his proximity, closing my eyes. Breathing slowly, I prepare my mind to shield me from the punishment I'm about to endure.

Except, when his hand reaches me, I'm not met with violence. Leo pulls me close, cradling me against his solid chest, chin resting atop my head, as if I'm a precious object.

"You've endured a miserable existence with one of the worst men in New Promise; that life is over. I know it will take time for you to believe me, but I have no intention of harming you. Please trust that you are safe with me." He holds me securely against him, and I listen to his heartbeat—steady, rhythmic, entrancing.

While I'm not positive his claims are true, the warmth of his embrace is endearing, dangerously so. No matter how convincing his actions seem, I must stay alert and keep my training at the forefront of my mind. Falling for his deceit could prove fatal.

Rising to my feet, I dust myself off and pat my hair down, hoping it's as neat as it was before. He stands, and another small tremor shakes my body from his nearness. Fortunately, he doesn't acknowledge it. Extending a bent elbow to me, he nods as I link my arm through it, and we make our way back into the main altar room.

The entire community is still present, and by the grins on the men's faces, they all believe he's claimed me. Replacing my well-practiced mask, I unlink our arms to stay one step behind him, as rule two dictates—a woman exists only in her husband's shadow.

"Esteemed Mr. Koeler, I must thank you for getting this waste of resources out of my home. She's been a problem her whole life," Raymond says as we approach him. Short, gruff, and unpleasant by nature, it's difficult to believe he's my father.

Behind him is my mother. Auburn hair, blue-green eyes, I was born a near-perfect copy of her. We're of the same short, slender build, gentle but strong-natured. Our only difference is that I am not yet soured by a lifetime of enduring my father, nor could I imagine loathing my own child as she does.

"Sir, your daughter is a lovely woman. I'm eternally thankful to you for accepting my gracious offer for her hand," Leo replies with an edge I haven't previously experienced. His hand finds my lower back, and I'm overcome with unexpected warmth.

Part of me foolishly believes he's not putting on an act in this moment.

When I was informed that a man had approached my father and offered to trade for my hand in marriage, I was in disbelief, but excited. Getting away from my father's wrath is a dream come true.

But in New Promise, a marriage may be a nightmare in the making.

I'll have to wait and see what comes of this.

As we pass through the crowd, several of my already-married acquaintances stand with their husbands. I haven't seen them since our final lesson. While I know this is common, it has been difficult.

When you spend nearly two decades together, being taught essential skills every woman must know, and proper behavior, you tend to grow close—as I did with Helena. She has a way of making me feel better after a particularly rough night with my father. Not having her support over these last few months has made his hatred difficult to bear.

Raymond's cruelty grows by the day, calling me a failure for not having a suitor the instant I turned twenty-one. Now, she stands sheepishly behind Brock, her cobbler husband. He's a tall blond man with vibrant blue eyes, in stark contrast to her tanned skin tone, rich brown eyes, and raven-black tresses. She meets my gaze for a moment, both of us forgetting our manners, and I dart my attention away as she does the same.

Hopefully, nobody noticed our blatant misbehavior.

Leo carries on, shaking hands and receiving small mementos from the other men as we make our way toward the exit. Foolishly, my curiosity takes over, and I spare him a glance. It's risky stepping out of line like this, but the indifference on his face as he pockets yet another meaningless bauble confuses me.

The weddings I've attended since coming of age have all been far more lively. New husbands emerge from the ceremony chamber with vibrant, proud smiles—having claimed their wives wholly. This feels somber and awkward.

Whether or not the rumors about Leo are true, I'm bound to him now, for however long that may be.

My head spins, and I stumble slightly. Gasps echo through the room as I regain my footing. Halting his steps, Leo turns my way, and I tuck my chin against my chest, preparing for public discipline.

"That's twice now she's made a mockery of him. A historian deserves an obedient and proper wife," a man in the crowd declares over the low murmurs.

"Disrespectful, that's what she is. Lowly daughter of a refuse man. How could she ever bear a proper son for him?" a different man—who I'm fairly certain is a farmer—says.

"Indeed, have her executed, and you can wed my daughter in three years, Koeler. She's properly behaved," another offers.

Placing a finger under my chin, Leo's eyes dance across my face as he lifts my head. He takes in the crinkle between my brows, attention then traveling to the chapped corner of my lip, the one that often falls victim to my teeth as I attempt to silence the static in my mind.

I avoid his gaze, just as I was taught, and bow my head in his hold, signaling my acceptance of the impending punishment.

Instead of a lashing, Leo rights himself, pulling me to his side before addressing the mob that has formed around us. "Phoebe is *my* wife. Let the record show that I could not care less what you expect of yours, but you will *not* lecture me on the ways I should treat mine. Have I made myself clear?"

Faces lose their color. Pompous expressions fall, leaving slack jaws and wide eyes in their wake.

"Do I need to explain more simply for the less intelligent citizens of New Promise?" Leo asks, deep voice resonating off the marble walls. "My wife will not be subject to this foolery. The etiquette rules and expectations will not apply to her under my roof. I will ensure she remains respectful while not in our private dwelling. However, that is where I draw the line." He releases his hold on me and strolls slowly, shoulders squared, to a gray, older man wearing a deep blue tunic. I immediately recognize him as one of our tailors, a rather miserable individual.

Leaning in, Leo's tall form looms over the stocky man. "If you *ever* suggest I execute her again, I'll kill you where you stand. My job, my status in the community, are of far greater value than your own. How *dare* you offer unsolicited advice on how to handle my personal affairs?" He straightens, readjusts his tunic, and stalks back toward me as the tailor trembles where he stands.

"S-sorry. My apologies for disrespecting you," the old man sputters.

The fire in Leo's eyes dissipates as he steps to my side, but the one that has roared to life in my veins burns with blazing force. He ushers me out of the altar building, and we immediately begin our trek to his—no, our—home.

I fall in line just behind him, but he slows, and I'm unsure of his intentions. We stop, and he reaches around to place his hand on my lower back, an action I still don't understand. This is irregular behavior, I was not trained for this. He uses light pressure to guide me to his side, leaving his hand in place as we resume our journey.

Our dusty, gloomy village is still and empty, as usual after a wedding. The rest of New Promise is likely celebrating in the Altar room, husbands boasting about their jobs, wives sitting in silence, tending to their needs. We're truly alone as we stroll casually along the stone path.

Would it be worth the punishment to ask him why he insists I walk beside, not behind, him?

No, definitely not. Surely I'm already on thin ice after the mishaps during our ceremony.

I could ask without anyone hearing. But if Leo isn't serious about not enforcing etiquette, then I'll pay the price for my curiosity—for daring to question my husband.

It's evening now, and the air has taken on its familiar chill. History books mention seasonal shifts in the weather, depending on how close the planet is to the sun, but that doesn't happen nowadays. Year-round, the temperature is fairly consistent—balmy warmth during the day, never quite seeing the full light the sun has to offer. Nights are cooler, not unbearably so, but enough that sleeping with blankets is required. Based on my limited knowledge, it is rather peculiar that no natural vegetation grows here, except for the greenery along the border walls. The environment works for curated crops, it's strange that wild plants never encroach.

"You're trouble," Leo speaks up with a faint chuckle, and I jolt at the unexpected sound. "Easy, Darling, I didn't mean to startle you. I had hoped the stories of your father were merely exaggerated musings of drunkards. Based on your reactions, they are factual as ever. You're more of a shell than the other women, which is a shame. I do hope in time you'll grow to trust me, at the very least."

Chewing my lip, I remain silent and continue. The thin fabric of my tunic allows me to feel the heat of his hand and the flexing of his fingers against my back.

"We're alone, speak to me," he commands.

"Why?" my voice squeaks out, just above a whisper.

"Because I live a lonely life, I would enjoy some conversation."

My brows knit together. "But... you choose to seclude yourself."

"You would be correct. I have my reasons, most of which have everything to do with my... situation." He clears his throat as we pass by the last cluster of common dwellings. Identical structures, made of gray stone that matches the barrier walls surrounding New Promise, the only abundant material we have now.

"Are we not going to your home?" I ask, wincing at my recklessness.

"We're going to *our* home. We don't live in the common area."

Right, ours.

He doesn't explain further, and I don't dare to ask. Historians are very peculiar, as the stories state. There are rumors he's particularly abnormal, and today's events have more than confirmed such. Several of the women in my group believe Leo is hiding something nefarious. It will be a disappointment if true, he's an attractive man and, at a glance, presents himself as kinder than most. I'm sure many of the women in New Promise would be happy to lie with him.

The faint pathway we're on veers left through an overgrown arch in the foliage. Leo ducks below the hanging vines, and I gasp at the scene that welcomes us on the other side.

"Welcome home, Phoebe Koeler." He removes his hand from my back, and I spin around, admiring the view.

We're in a secluded chamber of sorts. What appears as merely unkempt ivy on the bordering wall, in reality, houses a wondrous haven. Greenery, like nothing I've seen before, lines the columns, climbing toward the beams of sunlight breaking through the open top. Peering to the left and right, I realize that the walls surrounding

New Promise are double-layered the whole way through. Just far enough apart to allow a few people to fit comfortably. He has some sort of garden set up off to one side, and a small flock of hens on the other.

"Wait, there's no roof? No doors? No beds?" I clasp my hands over my mouth, regretting the string of insulting questions.

Stupid, you know better.

Leo chuckles and smiles at me.

What?

"Through here, Darling." He moves a shrub aside, revealing a hatch in the ground. "Watch your step when entering. I need to have a mason come out and repair the first landing."

As the door opens, I'm met with a stone staircase, disappearing deep into the unknown.

And a choice.

Sensing my reluctance, Leo closes his eyes and breathes slowly. "This is our home. I'll do no harm to you. This is how all historians live. You'll understand once you're inside. I'll give you the tour when we get down there. You know what will happen if you run... I can't stop them." The last words come out as more of a plea.

He's right. I know he is.

Today has been a test of my courage more than anything. I've survived all this time at the mercy of my father, how bad can whatever awaits me down there be?

Minutes pass slowly as I gather the will to take that first fateful step.

Staring down into the dark, I'm overcome with a squeezing in my chest. It feels as though I'm being strangled from the inside. Fogginess fills my head, and I struggle to stay upright as the vice around my lugs tightens further. Leaning against the cool stone wall, I slip to the ground and see Leo spring into action just as everything goes dark.

A sweet, nutty aroma fills the air around me. A hint of tartness, maybe a berry, accompanies the smell.

"Phoebe, are you awake?" Leo's voice filters into my head, almost forcing my eyes open.

Where am I? Why am I *comfortable*?

I'm in a bed?!

Run. Get out.

"Hey," he says softly, interrupting my inner quarrel. "I promise I will not harm you. Here." He hands me a plate filled with nuggets of toasted bread, smeared with different jams and nut butters. "You likely haven't ever had a good meal. Please enjoy. Once you've finished, I'll give you a tour of our home. " He takes a seat in the chair opposite the bed.

Sitting up, I do as instructed. Only, while I had planned to simply eat a few bites in compliance, the flavors that dance across my tongue with the first nibble pull a groan from my throat.

Curling my lips into my mouth, I drop the piece of bread and dip my head. "I apologize for my disturbance. It won't happen again, Ma—uhm, Leo." Wrenching my hands together, my stomach twists painfully.

When I lift my attention to him, I'm unsure how to decipher his body language. He's leaning back in the chair, one leg crossed over the other, hands holding an old-looking tome. Just now, I notice he's changed out of his marital tunic and is wearing deep-brown fitted trousers and an emerald-green button-down shirt. His sleeves are rolled up to his elbows, and he's simply reading, unbothered by my misbehavior.

"Are you not upset by my outburst?" I shrink further into myself, shaking my head in silent criticism of my continued carelessness.

"Upset about what, exactly? I quite like hearing you enjoy yourself. One day, I hope to witness *many* more of your sounds of pleasure. Once I've earned the right to draw them out of you." He peers at me over his book. Casually, he turns the page, eyes relaxed but filled with heated promise.

"Y-you want me to enjoy... it." My cheeks flush at the concept. If we were any other couple, we'd have already been intimate. I have no reason to be so timid around the subject. We study it at length for a reason, a woman has to know how to please her husband—it's our primary purpose in life—rule number one.

"I'm not your father, nor am I the majority of the male population of New Promise. Perhaps it's thanks to my studies, perhaps it's because I don't believe a woman is merely a vessel for our carnal desires as they all do. Regardless of the 'why'—" He sets the book down, uncrosses his legs, and leans forward. With his elbows resting on his knees, he addresses me directly, heavy gaze boring into my being. "—when I'm finally granted your consent to treat you as a husband *should* treat his wife, it will be my only objective to ensure you *thoroughly* enjoy every moment."

"W-why?"

"Because you're the most remarkable woman to have graced our generation, and likely the most intelligent in several."

His declaration gives me pause. I pull my head back, furrowing my brows. "You must be mistaken. I'm the least valuable woman in all of New Promise."

"Are you aware of the fact that no other woman in the last sixty years has shown the same curiosity and propensity to thrive, and purely survive, as you? To the majority, you're the daughter of a nobody, a drunkard with anger issues who was condemned to the bowels of our city. He hauls refuse for a living because anything else would be too complicated. But you, you've overcome the hardship being his daughter has brought. In your formative years, you were reprimanded time and time again for overstepping and asking questions that weren't meant for you. Yet, it took years for them to break you. Even now, I see sparks of curiosity in your eyes. Sparks, I'll nurture and transform into a blazing wildfire when you're ready."

"Uh." I avoid his eyes.

"Why do you think your mind goes dark on you as it did earlier? I'll tell you if you'd like to know the truth." He leans back in the chair, resting his hands on the arms at his sides.

My eyes widen, sweat instantly coats my palms. "You... know?"

"Yes. Just as it's doing at this very moment, your mind doesn't know what to do with all the questions and emotions flooding it. Instead of simply asking and allowing yourself to explore your curiosity, you've been conditioned to contain it. This has led to ancient ailments known as 'anxiety' and 'panic attacks'. Modern humans don't suffer from these because they've been mentally dulled through generations. You're a beautiful anomaly,

Darling." He smiles warmly at me. "So, when you feel like this, just ask. Feed that curiosity. I'll do my absolute best to answer."

"You *want* me to ask questions?" I shake my head again.

"Yes. But first, I want to watch you finish your meal so we can get you acclimated." He nods at my toast and picks up his book.

Lightness washes over me as I return to my food, 'panic' forgotten.

What waits for me once the plate is empty may just be the start of the rest of my life. One I could learn to enjoy.

S tepping out of the plain bedroom, I stop in the hallway. Once again, I spin in a slow circle and take in the wonder surrounding me.

"I've never been in a dwelling like this," I say, my voice meek as I follow Leo down the hall, dragging my hand along the stone wall. My fingertips tingle as they trail over the cool, slightly rough surface.

"Undoubtedly. This is not your ordinary home. Historians' chambers are ancient, passed down from generation to generation. It is why we are only permitted to raise sons." His meaning doesn't escape me.

Much like the Guides and their guards, historians must retain continuous bloodlines. Daughters are not an option. Any that may be born are taken at birth and passed on to the orphanage, raised in seclusion. Most end up as concubines for the Guides; others are married off. Whichever the Guides see fit.

Leo opens a solid wooden door to the right, and I find a restroom. These walls are adorned with sculptures and parchments featuring art and designs from ages long past. There's an entire set-up here with working plumbing, complete with a large bathtub and a separate shower chamber.

"Wow!" I step into the room and stretch my arms out. "I can't touch the walls! Does the tub work, and am I allowed to use it?" Instinctively, I clamp my mouth shut and contain the bubbling excitement.

"Phoebe," Leo addresses me softly, slipping his forefinger under my chin in the way I'm becoming increasingly fond of. Slight pressure lifts my face toward him. "It works, and you can use it any time you like." He rubs his thumb softly over my chin before lowering his hand. For a breath, I find myself yearning for more of his gentle touch. After considering me for a moment, he offers a curt nod and guides me out of the room.

Tracing the places he caressed, I march along behind him. The hallway opens into a rather large common room. A polished wooden dining table with four chairs sits in the center. To the right is a seating area, featuring a large piece of furniture I'm not familiar with. To the left is a kitchen, more extravagant than I'm accustomed to. Leo has stepped away for a moment, giving me time to inspect the cooking amenities.

"How will I prepare food down here? Where does the smoke from the fire go?" I walk toward the wooden counters and run my fingers across the polished marble top. Its patterns are intricate and different from the regular stone in most dwellings.

"You don't have to cook for me, I'm capable," Leo replies quietly.

The closeness of his voice sends a shiver through my body. He's *right* behind me, and I don't quite understand the fuzzy feeling in my stomach. Inhaling through my nose, I lay my hands flat on the surface before me and brace myself.

If he's going to force himself on me, surely it won't be on a counter, right?

"You look even more beautiful in our home," he murmurs, "I—" He clears his throat. "—Someday, I'd like to kiss you while we cook meals together."

I let out a held breath, ragged and hot.

This is it, steady yourself.

Slowly, I turn to face him and fidget with the loose fabric at the front of my tunic. With my gaze lowered, I watch as his chest rises and falls slowly, startling as he rests his chin atop my head, carefully encircling me with his arms. "Sorry, I-I just wasn't expecting to be so taken with you. Having you here feels as if you were always supposed to be."

Falling back into my training, I remember rule number three—a woman must please her husband whenever he wishes, lest she be executed for non-compliance—and reach for his belt. To my surprise, he stops me, large hands carefully taking hold of mine.

"Not like this. Not yet. Some day I'll have you in every room of this house, if you wish for it. But I know you don't want *this*." He releases his hold and steps away from me. "To answer your question, the stove is electric, a luxury few have. Since historians live underground, we must have proper accommodations." He attempts to discreetly adjust the bulge in his slacks, but I notice. It would be impossible not to.

"I'm sorry." I pull at a loose thread on my tunic. "I'll please you, even if I don't want to. It's my du—"

"No, it's not," he interrupts, voice stern but not unkind. "I apologize for losing my good sense and trying to rush this. I want you to love me, not loathe me." Measured and flat, his declaration sounds nearly rehearsed.

Has he practiced for this?

"Love?" The word feels foreign as it leaves my lips.

"Yes, love used to be the driving force for marriages. Men and women—or in other instances, men and men, or women and women—would build strong emotional bonds before marrying. Relationships, that's what they called them. There were no trades for marriage, women had a say in who their husbands were. They went on these outings called dates and shared intimate moments together. Women *worked* too! The world used to be this wondrous thing. I-I want something like that. Since I first read about it, it's all I've desired. That's what makes you perfect." His voice wavers, growing more animated than I've heard it.

As if he remembered something, his posture straightens, and the brightness in his expression fades. "My apologies if that was an overwhelming amount of information. I was caught off guard by a sudden rush of emotions. It won't happen again."

Something is definitely off. Where did his confidence and cool composure go?

I laugh to myself. It is ludicrous to think I've known him long enough to learn his mannerisms. In time, I will, and I genuinely hope I'm able to relax around him. This concept of love sounds enjoyable. There are far less appealing men in the community. Leo is quite attractive compared to most, as if appearances matter.

I don't dare explain to him that we're taught about love and how marriage used to be, if only briefly—just enough to convince us it is wrong to feel such things. Instead, I decide that a change of topic is the best course of action.

"Will you show me how to use the stove?" I ask, and he immediately perks up.

"Oh, of course. But not until later. For the time being, we'll continue your walkthrough." He motions toward the seating area and I follow close behind him.

"What is this large piece of furniture? It is peculiar."

"This, Dearest, is called a sectional sofa, categorized by the corner and separate parts. This particular piece is believed to be over one thousand years old. They were popular in a time when families were allowed to have more than one child. Could you imagine? How amazing would life be with a couple of children, gathering together on this cozy picture of comfort and sharing the events of your day?" A soft expression crosses his face.

My stomach fills with strange flutters, and I find myself smiling back at him. "I enjoy the deep blue shade. The fabric looks very plush and comfortable. May I sit on it?"

"You may, any time you wish. Eventually, I'd like to sit on it together, and someday possibly try cuddling on it." He offers a slight grin, tucking his hands into the pockets of his pants.

"What is cuddling?" I tip my head with a quirked brow. The word has never come up in all of our schooling. It feels forbidden to ask, and exciting.

"When people were in relationships, they would often seek physical affection from their loved ones. I've read many books about it, and the concept seems comforting. It's nothing more than laying with your bodies against one another." His face takes on a reddish color. For a moment, I think he's angry, but I'm fairly certain he's blushing.

I'm also *definitely* certain that I like it.

"You would want to do that?"

"Only if you wish." The redness of his cheeks deepens, and he shies away from my gaze. "Uh, I need to use the restroom. Allow me a moment, and I'll return to show you the rest of your new home." He hurries off to the hallway, and I take the opportunity to admire the decorations in the room.

More intricate carvings and parchments line the stone walls here. Most are nondescript and bear nothing of interest. However, one in particular catches my eye. A man and woman, embracing one another, lips meeting. They look peaceful, at ease in each other's arms. A strange ache resonates in my chest.

"Studying kissing techniques?"

I whip around to face Leo, having not heard him enter the room.

"Humans used to be much more unreserved with their emotions and affection." He steps next to me and places his hand on my lower back. "I apologize for leaving in such a manner."

"You don't need to apologize. I was simply admiring the decorations. I have heard of kisses, just never imagined them appearing so enjoyable. The few you've given me have been as such, despite the fact that you've yet to kiss me on the lips."

"Yes, well, we no longer partake in anything that could cause emotional fluctuations, and kissing falls into that category... especially on the lips. As for the tapestries and sculptures, when you live underground and have no windows, you must find other things to fill the space. Stone is only so appealing. Now, onto the final part of your tour." The familiar pressure of his hand steers me in the direction of another hallway.

On the wall are about a dozen pictures of the same couple. A tall man with dark skin, hair black as night, and gentle eyes. Next to him is a short blonde woman boasting a vibrant smile. Their arms are around each other in nearly every one, and they look... happy.

"Those are my parents. I like to keep pictures of them around as a reminder of love and happiness." He traces a finger along the frame of the largest one before guiding me the rest of the way.

Two doors occupy the walls across from one another, and a third at the very end. Large and wooden, solid as the rest.

"To the left, you'll find my bedroom, across the hall is the door to my study and the catacombs. You may enter. However, be warned, it's dark and not particularly entertaining."

"What are the catacombs for? I've never heard of such a word."

"Well, the top room is lined with tomes and things of the sort, the stairwell leads to the storage room of discovered materials I protect and catalog for New Promise."

"So, that's truly your job then? How do you trade for things? This electricity is expensive to produce, correct?" My face scrunches, head filled with static as I struggle to comprehend.

"Do you know how many people love useless things? Your father, for instance, traded your marriage rights for an ancient silk pillow. As for the lights, the Guides ensure all historian homes stay powered. One of the few perks of such a tedious job," he explains as though it's simple.

"A... pillow." I lurch my head back, scowling intensely.

"It was his price. He was honestly more amazed that someone showed interest in your hand. The fool." A crooked grin pulls at his face, and my breath catches.

His trip to the bathroom seems to have fixed the uncertainty he had been suffering from. This is the correct version of Leo. Sure of himself, slightly brash and direct, it's comforting in an odd way.

"So, what about the other door?" I ask, not yet ready to linger in his presence.

"That, Darling, is my single rule for you. You must never, under any circumstances, open that door. Can you promise me you'll stay far away from that room?" His voice lowers, eyes locking with mine. The warning is clear, but not malevolent in nature, only serving to confuse me further.

Frozen in place, my pulse quickens. Prickles line the back of my neck. I have no choice but to agree. Something about how serious he is convinces me that there is nothing good behind that door. He may not want to harm me, but I have enough wit to understand that what lies on the other side will.

Still, I can't move.

"Phoebe. Hey," he says in a gentle tone. "I didn't mean to upset you. Just, please don't open the door. Okay?" The softness returns to his face, and I feel my body let go of the tension.

"Okay." I finally manage a faint nod.

"Well then, go and run yourself a bath. You've taken in a lot of information today and deserve a breather. I'll make dinner while you decompress. I'll show you how everything functions starting tomorrow. There's no stress and no timeline—no pressure to do, or be, anything other than yourself."

He leads the way back to the bathroom and shows me how the knobs work to set the water at my preferred temperature before leaving me to relax.

As I sink into the lavender-scented bath, courtesy of the nice soap my family could never afford, I feel the urge to cry. Why? I'm not sure. The only thing I've managed to learn today is that Leo Koeler is as peculiar as the rumors make him out to be.

Whether that peculiarity will be good or bad for me is still unknown. A portion of my subconscious hopes for the best. For the first time in my life, things just may work out.

4

Waking up here is surreal. The stories shared in our training program still filter through my mind. Of all the things I was prepared to face—voracious sexual appetites, being forced to scrub floors with my bare hands, having to spend my waking minutes tethered to my husband, ready to fulfill his every whim, knowing how to cook several of our common dishes—I was not told how to deal with sleeping alone, wondering when I'm permitted to leave my room, how soon to prepare breakfast when I'm not instructed to do so. It's quite the conundrum.

Throbbing in my temples blurs my vision. Did he intentionally set me up to fail? Is he waiting on the other side of my door, eager to reprimand me?

My fears nearly come to fruition as a knock echoes through the room. Pulling the bedsheets to my chest, I tuck my knees up and brace myself.

Leo enters a moment later, already clothed for the day. Another pair of well-fitted slacks, charcoal in color, frame his long legs. Matching his pants is a vest, the cinch accentuating his trim waist. Wide and powerful, his shoulders almost seem out of place, but add a pleasant shape to the overall silhouette as his shirt, the color of a night sky, strains to contain them. Simply put, he's statuesque.

"Guide's mercy, are you cold?" he asks with a faint gasp. "I can adjust the temperature of the climate controls if need be."

"N-no." My response is nearly silent as I fight the urge to run.

"Why on earth are you curled up on the edge of your mattress? Is it not satisfactory?" He makes a move to come closer, and I flinch. "Oh, I understand. Please, Dearest, do not fear me. I've come to ask if you're feeling well enough to learn some things."

"What sort of things? I'd like to learn how to operate the stove."

"If that is where you wish to begin, surely I can accommodate. Meet me in the kitchen when you're ready." He nods and leaves the room, clicking the door shut behind him.

Scurrying to my feet, I rush to the closet where my minuscule selection of tunics is now stored. I run my fingers over the rough fabric and sigh.

They're clean, at the very least, but that does nothing for the horrendous quality. Each is a different shade of brown, the least flattering—and thus cheapest—color one can buy. I choose the one that feels least callous on my skin, securely tie it around my waist, and make haste toward the kitchen.

Leo's features flash with shock as I enter the room. "What are you wearing?" he asks, face contorting strangely.

"A... tunic." I stare down at the ill-fitting fabric. "I chose my nicest one, is it not satisfactory?"

"Dearest, I know the law only allows women to wear these ridiculous things, but is this scrap comfortable? Shall I send for a tailor to fit you for new ones?" He steps away from the counter and approaches me. "You're being engulfed by this wretched fabric."

I shudder when his hand moves to my collar. "It's all my father would purchase for me. I've had the same seven for the past few years. If it does not please you, I will remove it." Moving my hands to the frayed ties, I begin to undo the knots.

"Guides no. My intention is not to make you uncomfortable or inconvenience you. I merely wish to care for you. Please allow me to send for higher-quality tunics. You deserve comfort."

I look to his face and see a softness I've not known another man to possess. His defined cheekbones stain pink under my inspection.

"May I show how to operate the stove as you requested?" He dips his head and turns away from me to begin fumbling with the dials. "These are all labeled. You simply push in and turn to your desired temperature. Unlike the fire-based stoves in most dwellings, these electric ones allow you to have greater control over the heat levels at which you cook."

I watch dutifully as he reaches into a top cabinet. The stretch causes his shirt to untuck, and I'm given a glimpse of his lower abdomen. A scattering of dark hair draws my attention to his waistband, where it disappears into his slacks. Unfamiliar heat rises to my cheeks as my attention lingers. Strange tingles fill my body, but not the way they do when I'm about to have a panic attack.

Placing the pan he retrieved on the stove, he then readjusts his shirt. "Would you like some eggs?" he asks, facing away from me as he turns to the food storage box. Examining it closer, I noticed it is filled with ingredients I can not name, it is also larger than those I've seen, and it seems to be... cold?

"Would you prefer vegetables instead? Do you have food preferences?" He spins around with an armful of unrecognizable items. I stand wide-eyed, and he tilts his head. "Have you never seen fresh rations before?"

"I have not. Fresh food is a luxury that my father's status does not provide," I mumble.

"We have a garden up top, as I'm sure you noticed. I read in history books about how ancient farmers tended to their crops and propagated some of my favorite vegetables from remnants of rations. Perhaps we could expand it to include some of your favorites as well. If you'd like." He offers a timid smile, eyebrows slightly raised.

"I'm afraid I have little experience with vegetables to offer an opinion." I chew my lip as my shoulders fall.

"Not to worry, we'll try a large variety over time. I do have a small flock of hens that I was able to barter with a farmer for, they supply a sufficient amount of eggs." He beams, abundantly proud of his accomplishments.

Our conversation flows with such ease that I want to believe the things he's promising. Boldly, I offer a faint smile in return, and his face somehow fills with more joy.

"Would you like to cook breakfast with me?" he asks, placing some greenery on the counter alongside a few eggs. I step next to him and lift one, admiring the texture of the rich brown shell. "Have you only ever eaten dehydrated eggs, Dearest?"

His voice is soft, surely aware of my answer before I speak it.

"That is correct. They are also a luxury. I know what they look like, but holding one feels like a special gift."

"Try this, let me know if you enjoy it." He lifts a bit of the greenery to my mouth, and I take it eagerly. My lips brush against his fingertips as I do, and his breath falters.

"My apologies," I respond immediately around the delicious bite.

"You're quite alright. Please tell me what you think of the pepper." He clears his throat and tucks his hands into his pockets.

I savor the crisp vegetable, enjoying the flavorful juices as they burst in my mouth. Bright, slightly spicy, *fresh*. I chew longer than necessary before responding, "That was delicious. I've had dried peppers in my ration boxes, but had no idea they were so crisp and juicy when fresh." I bounce lightly on my feet, excited by the concept of all the new foods I'll be trying.

"Well, peppers are some of my absolute favorites, so there are plenty more where that came from. I'm sure to keep a few seeds, so I have them in constant supply." He chops more and adds it to the pan. It makes a sizzling sound as he taps eggs on the edge of a bowl.

"How may I be of assistance?" I ask, eager to serve him, and guided by a hint of my own excitement to try the foods he's promising.

"Would you kindly whisk these until they're fully incorporated?" He hands me the bowl and a fork.

With a genuine smile on my face, I proceed to break the yolks and mix. I don't mind cooking, not really. I had primarily dreaded the thought of preparing dry rations for a husband who expected *more*. But this? Something as menial as making eggs and peppers *with* my husband... It's enjoyable. Sharing our time, working together on tasks, and engaging in casual conversation while we prepare delicious-smelling food. I could see myself adjusting to a life like this.

Leo reaches over and extends his hand, interrupting my musing. I pass him the *thoroughly* whisked eggs, courtesy of my mind wandering, and he pours them into the pan. I watch him slide them around with the peppers, and they slowly solidify into something more familiar.

"Here." He scoops out a portion and blows on it. "I added some seasonings; there's a large collection of salt rocks, and they liven up every meal. I quite enjoy fresh chives as well, so I mixed in some of those."

Was I that distracted?

The creamy, golden spoonful in front of me smells herbaceous and zesty. I open my mouth, and he gently feeds me the sample. As the flavors mingle, I groan, surprised by the savory perfection. Dried rations could never compare to this. The texture is softer and more velvety than I've ever experienced. I lick my lips, savoring the taste, and Leo's eyes lock onto them.

He clears his throat and returns his focus to the cupboard, setting out two plates. "It's to your liking, I presume?" he asks, scooping out a sizable portion.

"It is the best thing I've ever tasted," I answer honestly. "May I have some more?"

He stops, mid-scoop, and blinks. As he turns in my direction, his brows pinch together. "You can have anything you wish. Please consider everything in this home yours, just as much as it is mine. You needn't ask permission to enjoy your home."

"Except for the secret room." I go still as the words linger in the air. "I-I apol—"

"No, there's no apology necessary. What I have secured behind that door will be yours too someday, should you prove that I can trust you with the information it conceals." He works his jaw, inhaling through his nose. "If you could be privy to the truth now, I would gladly take you there in an instant. But I need to trust in your devotion and discretion." He dishes out the rest of my portion and hands me the plate. "Now, we shall eat together before I must excuse myself. The work of a historian is demanding, and I must stay on schedule."

"What is it that you do, exactly?" I ask as I take a heaping bite of eggs. All of my etiquette training vanishes the instant I taste it again. He watches me with admiration, entranced by the way I eat in the least cultured way possible.

A soft chuckle leaves him before he answers, "I have many duties, most of which include cataloging ancient items, maintaining knowledge of civilizations past, consuming ancient scripts, and re-penning them for the Guides."

"So, you work for the Guides?" My mouth falls open, fork clanging against the plate as it drops out of my hand.

"In an indirect way, yes. Historians, for as many generations as we can remember, have assisted the Guides in safeguarding pivotal information for our continued survival. This is how I know the proper way to garden and how to care for the hens. Even in the instance that I have no tasks assigned to me, I must stay vigilant in expanding my knowledge. It is also why, should you ever desire a child, we are only permitted to raise a son, so that he may carry on my legacy."

"So," I scrunch my face, pulling my lips to the side. "If the world died and took all life forms with it, how are there plants? How do we have chickens and livestock? Also, forgive me for speaking out of turn, but am I understanding correctly that you will not force me to bear your child?"

"Those," he exclaims, leaning forward to rest his chin on his hands. "Are the exact type of questions that tell me you were the right choice for a wife. I have my theories... Someday, when you're ready, I'll enlighten you. I will also never force anything onto you. For now, Dearest, I must tend to my duties. Do feel welcome to join me in the catacombs, should it interest you." He wipes his mouth and stands to take his dish to the sink.

As he makes his way down the hallway, I feel a sense of emptiness take hold. The room is less vibrant now, and I wonder if he feels the same with the lack of my presence.

My first official day as the wife of Leo Koeler has been... enlightening. My life is vastly more interesting than I am accustomed to, that much is certain.

I 've been here for several days now, to the point
I've lost track, and Leo has been an interesting husband. Having first-hand experience, I fully understand the rumors. I've determined he's
not *quite* stable—what with the mood changes
and all. The fact would normally cause alarm and
put me in a mindset to be more cautious around
him, should he have a darker side I've yet to meet.
But, beyond the threat to kill that old tailor, he's
never once shown any violent tendencies, regardless of the version of him I get.

While Leo has left me to my own devices for
the majority of my stay here thus far, he has not
once forbidden me from accompanying him in his
duties.

Today, I have every intention of joining him.

We've just concluded our daily breakfast, and
I'm working in the garden. Not because he told me
to, but because I enjoy tending to the plants. The

hens have also grown quite fond of me and now eagerly approach the barrier that contains them as I arrive.

Such peculiar creatures. Their quiet clucks are a comfort I hadn't expected, and the vegetable scraps from our breakfast always perk them up. After sprinkling some around their enclosure, I make my way to their nests and collect the eggs.

"Six! You ladies have been quite busy." I chuckle. "We shall enjoy your gifts, as always." After patting each of them on the head, I step out of the enclosure and make quick work of getting inside.

Our home is quiet, as usual. We're far enough removed from the heart of New Promise that the sound clutter is nonexistent. Serenity, that's what it is. Not having to hear all our neighbors and their theatrics is a blessing.

The Powers Above truly seem to have smiled upon me.

With an unnatural bounce in my step, I nearly skip to the far hall, stopping at the study door. Should I knock? Would he hear it if I did? I've never been inside, what awaits me could be anything. Catacombs, what are they? In conversation, Leo makes them sound large and wondrous, so surely he'd never hear a knock at the door if he's down there.

Carelessly, I open it and, as he detailed, find a small study on the other side.

Shelves line the far wall, filled with weathered tomes and scrolls from ages long gone. Trinkets and large sculptures adorn the side wall—silver weapons of sorts, a suit of metal armor, some country tapestries I've never seen. There is even a large sculpture that looks like the Earth, at least from what I've seen in history books.

At the back of the room, Leo sits in an armchair next to a polished wooden side table piled high with tomes. His pose is reminiscent of that from my bedroom the day we married. Right leg crossed over the left as he intently studies the book in his right hand. A drinking glass, half-filled with an unfamiliar amber liquid, cradled in his left.

"My apologies for interrupting. I was not expecting you to be in here." I breathe out, dipping my head as I turn to excuse myself.

"Your presence will never qualify as an interruption, Darling." Attention shifting to me, he takes a slow sip. "Do come sit with me." He motions to a mustard-colored plush chair next to him with a gentle smile.

As I approach, his gaze sweeps over me, as if he hadn't noticed my new tunic at breakfast.

"Please forgive me for staring. You're stunning when wearing properly fitted clothing, Phoebe," he murmurs, eyes lazily hooded.

"You have the right to admire your wife," I respond in a neutral tone as I move to sit.

"Does it cause you discomfort knowing that I find you unreasonably attractive?" He closes his book and addresses me directly.

"Truthfully, no. You've been extremely respectful. Thank you for your continued consideration of my feelings." I maintain eye contact with him, despite my mind protesting in the name of marriage rule seven—be submissive at all times, never challenge your husband's authority.

"You've adjusted quite well thus far. It pleases me to see you enjoying your days." He nods faintly and returns to his studies.

We sit in comfortable silence for several moments. He occasionally glances at me over the pages, and I watch as his brows lift and furrow while he reads.

Curiosity finally wins, and I speak up, "I had assumed the catacombs would be much more expansive."

"They are, this is just my study, remember? There's a hatch that leads down to the historical archives I'm in charge of," he answers, nose buried in the pages.

"May I ask what you're reading?" I lean over, trying to get a look.

"In ancient times, scribes would write fictional love stories. I'm quite fond of them. This is a rather interesting one. The title is worn off the cover, but the pages are intact. The woman in this story is a childcare provider for the man. They're currently resisting a very obvious mutual attraction."

"So... you read stories about love?" I tip my head, attempting to gain a better view.

"Sometimes, yes. Would you care to sit with me and read along?" He uncrosses his legs and leans back, a silent invitation.

When I'm greeted with this side of him, my body nearly vibrates, begging to be closer. Where I find his more bashful tendencies endearing and alluring in their own right, this direct, commanding persona calls to my daring side.

Finally, I give in to his charm. His eyes flare as I rise to my feet and close the gap between us. Gaze soft and focused on me, his breathing slows as I maneuver myself onto his lap.

Adjusting below me, he wraps a strong arm around my waist and places his drinking glass on the desk. "Are you comfortable like this?" he asks, allowing his hand to linger on my hip.

Until now, I've never been close enough to experience his essence in the way I currently am. Warm and firm, I settle in as his rustic scent entrances me, smelling of linen and spices I cannot name.

My mouth feels as though I've swallowed sand.

"I am," I admit, finding myself too timid to look him in the eye.

"Wonderful, now shall I read to you? Be aware that there are... salacious scenes in some of these stories. If you become uncomfortable, be sure to tell me." He lifts the book and curls me into his chest.

As he narrates through several chapters, I draw distinct comparisons to our life together. How he flushed bright red as our fingers brushed while assisting me with breakfast preparations. The way his eyes glimmer when I enter the room. His joyous expression when he first showed me the hens. How gently he's holding me now, sharing this aspect of his duties with me.

"Leo," I interrupt with my hand tucked securely against him.

"Yes, Darling?" He drops his chin, resting it atop my head.

"Do you think you could love me like this?" I'm unsure why I ask, blame the way my heart stutters as he reads.

"I'd enjoy nothing more, as soon as you're ready for it." With a slow sigh, he resumes reading aloud. Eventually, I succumb to the blissful peace his presence brings and fall asleep.

"Dearest, I've made you something to eat. You've been resting for several hours now." Leo kneels at my bedside, waking me from the restful slumber

I had been lost in. He's changed into a different outfit, as he tends to do later in the day.

"Powers Above, is it time for dinner already? Having you read to me was more soothing than I could have anticipated." I sit up and stretch, tunic parting slightly.

"It pleases me to know you slept well, and that I played a part in your comfort." He smiles brightly, eyes drifting to the sliver of exposed skin on my chest before darting back to my face. "Do come eat with me. I'd quite enjoy your company." Face flushed, he stands and leaves me to finish waking.

After combing my hair and fixing my tunic, I make haste to join him at the table. Quite a spread awaits me as I sit. He's laid out more vegetables for me to try, some long and orange, and another has been broken down into a soft paste of sorts.

"What is this?" I ask as I stare at the centerpiece. The golden carcass, covered in herbs, smells delicious.

"It's a hen, I procured it from a farmer. Ours would not make for a great meal, they're far too old."

My shoulders slacken, the tension I had felt building releases as relief washes over me. "Guides' mercy, you nearly upset me for a moment."

"Not to worry, I have noticed how much you adore our flock. I would never do anything to upset you in such a way." He grabs a knife and slices into the succulent meat. Steam rises in plumes, wafting the spiced aroma through the room. "Would you like to try some vegetables with it?"

I nod quickly, eyes intently watching as he handles the knife with precision.

"Why are we feasting? What's the occasion?" I direct my attention to his face.

"Well, it has been two weeks since our wedding. It may seem menial, however, your progress is deserving of celebration." He scoops the white puree onto my plate alongside some of the orange vegetables. "This is a potato mash, and some carrots roasted alongside the hen," he explains, placing the dish before me.

"I don't feel as though I have accomplished anything noteworthy." I stare down at the plate and feel my mouth begin to water.

"You may not, but I do. You hardly try to revert to the things they taught you. You have found yourself a nice daily routine and taken a liking to gardening. It's been several days since you asked if I needed to be pleasured." Coupled with his praise, the grin on his face is infectious.

"Do you not require pleasing?" I lift my brows and tilt my head.

He nearly drops his knife. "I uh-well." A blush overtakes his face, and he clears his throat. "We all need pleasing, no?" His gaze locks with mine, and I swallow hard.

"Women know no pleasure," I drop my eyes to the table, fidgeting with my fork. Regret floods me in an instant.

"May I be forward with you?"

I look to him and, despite the ice in my veins, nod.

"The walls here are stone, they do a poor job of concealing sound. Even if you believe you're not making much at all."

I go straight as a board in my chair, sweat beads on my forehead and my stomach nearly hits the floor. "Please be merciful. I-I know it's impure to pleasure myself, it shall never happen again."

It's not only improper, but it also violates rule four—a man's pleasure is all that matters. Should a woman seek her own, outside of any provided by her husband, she may be subject to execution.

"Dearest, I believe you've misjudged my words. Please yourself as you wish, I do the same."

His confession stops my building worry in its tracks.

"You do? Should that not be my duty?"

"Some day when you're ready, it will be." His easy smile warms my insides.

"Do you... please yourself when you hear me?" I move my fork through the potato puree, avoiding his gaze. My pulse races in anticipation. The image in my mind is indecent at best.

A heated silence fills the space between us.

Eventually, I hear him blow out a heavy breath. "Would that upset you?" he asks, voice ragged.

"No," I whisper, flushed face still directed at my food. "Truthfully, I think I enjoy the notion."

A strangled sound leaves him, drawing my attention to his face. He sits across from me, eyes closed as he takes grounding breaths. "My apologies, I did not intend for our conversation to stray so far. My intentions were not inherently sexual. Forgive me?" His forehead wrinkles from the rise of his brows as he mimics a pout.

"There is no need to apologize, I'll be more mindful and quiet in the future."

"Please don't," he fires back instantly. "Uh, what I mean is..." He chews his lower lip, unable to find the words he's searching for.

"You find pleasure in hearing me enjoy myself? Just as you told me in my room the day we married," I offer in response, admittedly more direct than I should.

"Correct. I very much enjoy hearing you." He nods stiffly.

"Then I shall continue if it pleases you. We will both benefit." I beam at him and take a bite of my hen. "This is quite delectable. You're a wonderful cook. Thank you, Leo."

He stares at me, confusion clear as day on his face. "Y-you're welcome." He swallows a large gulp of water and skewers a chunk of carrot on his fork.

Casual conversation resumes as we continue to enjoy our meal. Once our plates have been cleared, I gather the dirty dishes and take them to the sink to wash them. Leo comes to my side and wipes them down, putting them away when they're dry. Once finished, we retire to our respective rooms for the evening.

As I prepare for bed, today's events echo through my mind. Falling asleep in Leo's arms, eating delicious food... even our slightly uncomfortable dinner conversation all make me appreciate this new life. Even if I'm still struggling to adjust to how strange he is.

One thing is certain, I've never known a man like Leo, and now that I have, I'm eager to learn more.

Walking confidently into the study, I'm greeted by a brightly smiling Leo. I've spent several hours here with him off and on over the last week. He reads me enchanting stories of love, war, epic battles, and devastation.

As I approach, he stands. "Are you done with the hens, Darling? I have something special in store for you today."

"And what might that be?" I ask, although I know he'll show me regardless.

He finds such joy in the fact that I share interests with him. The hens and garden are one thing, but my mutual enjoyment of his historian duties makes his cooler, more reserved side soften.

"Today, we're going into the catacombs."

Excitement rolls through me like electricity. I bounce on my toes jubilantly, causing him to chuckle.

"I know you've been eager to see and learn more. My apologies for waiting so long. I wanted to allow you time to get comfortable." A small smile remains on his face as he strolls past me. In the corner of the room, he finds a loose floorboard and lifts.

"You never mentioned that the hatch is concealed," I watch in awe as the portion of the floor opens with a faint creak.

So many secrets he still hides away, like whatever I hear rustling on the other side of that locked door when I'm near.

"There are sacred things stored here, of course it's concealed. Nothing of importance is left in the open." He motions for me to step inside, and I do so without hesitation.

He follows close behind, and we descend a long stairwell, clicking a light on to illuminate our way. The air feels damp, cooler—smelling slightly stale. Once we reach the bottom, there's nothing but an empty space. Stone carved directly from the Earth, not placed by hand like most of the dwellings in New Promise. This is a natural cavern of sorts, though definitely polished by tools.

The wonder and amazement I had been preparing for are nowhere to be found. My pulse quickens, skin getting strangely hot and cold at once. There's nothing here. Nothing but me and a practical stranger.

"L-Leo?" I ask as my mind races. "What is this? Is it because I went too close to the door? I won't try to listen to the movements again. I swear it." I turn to him, eyes darting around the room that may become my grave.

"Easy, Darling. It's just a decoy room. Please allow me a moment." He slips past me and presses a nearly indistinguishable stone on the wall. Rumbles vibrate the floor as it separates, revealing a previously concealed doorway.

"Wow," I gasp as my nerves settle.

"I didn't intend to scare you. You... you don't think I would harm you still, do you?" The faint crack in his voice lets his hurt slip through. Guilt gnaws at my stomach from the sound.

Foolish woman, you've upset him.

"My reaction was not intentional. You've done nothing to make me feel threatened. Please forgive me for my irrational fears. Men aren't exactly kind by nature, and I know I've stepped out of line." I drop to my knees and fold my hands together. "Please?"

"Darling, I do not care if you go near the door. I merely ask that you never open it. Curiosity is fine, but it can be deadly if allowed to wander too far. Please, let me show you some of my favorite items in my care." He reaches a hand out. With his assistance, I get back to my feet. He pulls me closer than I've ever allowed, throwing caution aside. "Phoebe, I want to love you, *really* love you. Your understanding of what that means will grow in time. But please, for my sanity, never assume I'll harm you again." His breath dances along my skin, just before he blinks away the intensity in his eyes and releases me.

He clears his throat and nods, motioning for me to follow. I steel my nerves, cooling the heat in my veins, and trail behind him into a chasm. It appears endless, fading to pure darkness. My eyes can't focus on any single item. Things I couldn't dream of naming are scattered about the space.

"This way." He leads me down a side corridor.

We enter a room filled with the skeletal remains of colossal beings. I stand slack-jawed in the center. "I had wondered why the staircase down here was so long. Are these real bones?" I whirl around to Leo, who is *right* behind me, face alight with excitement.

"They are," he confirms while spinning me back around and wrapping his arms around me.

With small touches, tucking stray hairs behind my ear whilst we cook, faint caresses while he reads to me, he's been increasing his physical affection over the past week. I find that I'm growing fond of it.

"These are referred to as dinosaurs. Hundreds of millions of years ago, these giants ruled the planet. Then, much like with humanity, there was a mass extinction. Speculation suggests a meteor caused an ecological collapse at that time, unlike the devastation humanity brought to the ecosystem. We caused our own destruction."

"They're majestic, do they have names?"

"Well, this one—" Hands finding my waist, he guides me to a skeleton on all fours, with long horns on its forehead. "—is called a Triceratops, and the one over there is a Tyrannosaurus. We also have a few Stegosaurus, but none are complete. Each of these was assembled down here generations ago. My family has been guarding these catacombs for the past seven." He releases his hold and strolls into the next room.

Eager to discover more wonders, I follow without instruction. I cross the threshold and, as expected, am awestruck and speechless.

"These are much newer fossils, of species lost in our collapse. Brave adventurers were tasked with traversing the wasteland outside our walls to obtain them." He stops at a majestic skeleton, four-legged and just a bit taller than him.

"This looks beautiful," I say, rendered nearly breathless.

"These were called horses; they were some of humanity's most loyal companions. Through the documents left by our first generation of collapse survivors, we know they accompanied us through wars and were trusty workers who had been helping humanity from the dawn of time." His eyes shine as he talks about the animals lost to our foolishness.

There are dozens of smaller skeletons assembled in the room, and he explains a brief history of each to me until I'm exhausted. As I yawn for the fourth time, he chuckles and concedes, taking me back through the maze of tunnels and guiding me to the comfort of our home.

"Go rest. I'll wake you for dinner in a few hours. If you need me before then, I'll be in my study. Thank you for enjoying your time with me." For a brief instant, he begins to lean in, intentions clear.

A flare of panic shoots through me, partnered with an odd electric feeling. His mind takes control of his body, shutting down his instincts, and he stops himself, granting me a slight smile as we stand at the threshold of my room.

"Thank you for sharing part of your life with me, Leo," I offer in return.

"I hope to share the rest of my life with you. Sweetest of dreams, Darling." Mind be damned, he lets his body lead the way this time. Gently, he presses his lips to my forehead, causing my legs to wobble despite the inclination to stiffen.

Sensations burst to life inside me, and I feel my chest flutter. My burning cheeks must be the response he is looking for, because his smile widens ever-so-slightly before stepping out of the room.

As I stroll to the kitchen, Leo is just beginning to prepare dinner. I watch him as he chops carrots and tosses them into a pot. He's relaxed and far more casual while cooking. Some of my favorite moments with him have happened in this kitchen. We share laughs and bashful glances as we prepare meals each day.

To think I would have done this all alone had I married any other man.

"What's the planned meal for tonight? How can I help?" I end my ogling and step next to him at the counter.

"Oh, you're awake! I'll always accept your company. If you'd like, you can cut these onions. Be warned that they will make your eyes water. So, if you'd rather not, I can handle them."

"I've graduated to finally being trustworthy enough to wield a knife?" I tilt my head at him, brow quirked.

"Dearest, it was never about you being trustworthy. I'm well-trained in hand-to-hand combat, and you are not a threat to me." He huffs out a laugh.

"Do you care to explain why I've been a whisk wielder up to this point, then?" I place my hands on my hips, and he turns toward me.

My confidence wavers until I find humor alight on his face. He mimics my stance, a smirk pulling tightly at the corner of his mouth. "I've seen your training reports. I know that knife skills are *not* your strong suit. If you'd like to disprove the information I was provided, please do so."

"They... grade our training progress and share it with you?" I gasp, scandalized by the concept. It's no secret that our skills are documented, so potential husbands can choose a wife suited to their specific needs. However, the fact that they are scored is never disclosed to us. Knowing the truth makes my blood run scalding hot.

"You weren't aware? All this time, I thought you knew. My apologies." His shoulders fall, playful jesting gone as a silent frustration takes its place.

"I-but... they said I was a bad cook? How preposterous!" I take hold of the knife and slice into the onion, cutting it in half as I've watched him do several times over these past weeks. Tears instantly sting my eyes, but I dice exactly as I was taught. In no time at all, I've completed the task and turn back toward him, beautifully prepared onion chunks on display.

He lets out a low whistle, admiring the pile. "I stand corrected. That was quite impressive."

"Cutting things when you have swollen eyes and fingers from being beaten senseless by your father is no easy task. Perhaps they should have graded my motor skills while I wasn't physically injured." I grunt, releasing previously unacknowledged anger.

He moves closer, opening his arms. I stand still, blinking away tears that have nothing to do with the onions, and nod in silent consent. Holding his breath, as if sudden movements will change my decision, he envelops me in his strong arms.

"You'll never know pain like that again." He squeezes gently, granting me comfort from his strength. "You're positive this is acceptable? We've not been this close before, but I felt a hug would be appreciated."

"I-I like this. You're warm, and the pressure is relieving. Please don't release me yet." My voice comes out hoarse, muffled by his chest where I've securely buried my face.

He says nothing, but continues to hold me as I calm the storm in my mind. I breathe deeply, noting the slight change in his scent. Linen still permeates my senses, but the spices are different. Perhaps it's because of the onions and herbs we've prepared. No matter the reason, I still can't seem to get enough. With a final inhale and slow exhale, I nod, and he releases me.

"Let's cook. I'm famished." I return to the counter, cheeks stained with tears, and begin chopping herbs while he places the onions in a heated pan.

"Thank you for trusting me to hold you in a time of emotional distress. I enjoy being a source of comfort for you," he murmurs while stirring in the chives I finished.

"I've never had a hug before, it was very calming. So, thank you, Leo."

He smiles over at me before adding squash to the mixture. "I bartered for some cream. We're making soup. I was wondering if you'd be interested in sipping it from mugs while we cuddle on the couch. If that's too forward, feel free to decline." His cheeks redden as he turns away.

"That sounds pleasant. I enjoy sitting with you as we read. What difference would the couch make? Some comforting soup would be nice as we enjoy each other's company."

"I could gather a book and read to you as we sit, if you'd like," he offers, voice pitched slightly higher with hope.

"I would enjoy that." I smile at him.

As we finish cooking, he pours our portions into two large mugs and hands them to me, then disappears to the study.

I move to the seating area, setting his dinner on the table next to the sofa before sitting with my own.

He returns moments later with two options in hand. "This one is a history book about the time before the collapse. The other is one of those love stories you like. Which would you prefer I read?"

"The love story! I adore them. Some day I want to feel love like the people in those books." I flash a bright grin at him and take my seat.

"In time, I hope we can find that together." He sits next to me, grabbing his mug, and I curl into his side.

Looking up at him as he begins the story, I try to envision loving him. I pay careful attention to the way he sips his soup and checks in with me as I listen to his silly voices for each character.

Something about reading out here on the couch fills him with a more childlike flair. In the study, he's more serious, no matter the subject we're reading, which is fitting for the setting, there he's in duty mode. This post-duty story time is enter-taining, and while I don't know how to process the feelings I do have, I can easily determine that they're all positive.

I may not love him now, but days like this make it feel like a definite possibility.

Today we're attending our first town meeting. As an unmarried woman, I've never been allowed. Now I'm deemed a worthy companion and must wear my finest clothes.

The problem is that I have none.

I'm sitting at the vanity table in my room—an ancient piece from the catacombs that Leo gifted me after I showed interest—brushing my hair as he approaches. Our eyes meet in the mirror, and the tenderness I find in his tells me what kind of interaction this will be.

Currently, I'm presented with the soft, more timid side of Leo. The one who wants to cuddle after dinner and help me with the dishes. The Leo who makes my heart beat irregularly with his tenderness. Where his more serious side has the same effects, this more playful, and dare I say loving, side does so in a much more subtle way.

Surprisingly, I'm growing to enjoy the faint touches, his small smiles as I share my excitement over food, the way his breath catches when I allow the happiness I'm discovering to shine through. On the other hand, when we're in the study, and he's more serious, I'm intrigued by how his softer edges harden, the way his mannerisms become more intentional. That is the version of him I had expected now, but this is a welcome surprise.

"I thought you were tending to your duties?" I turn in my seat and smile up at him as he steps beside me.

"I am. However, I wanted to check in and see how you're feeling about today." He sits in the old chair across from me and silently awaits my response.

"I know you'll be there, so the event itself isn't any concern of mine. Just, maybe don't threaten to kill a man this time." I let out a soft chuckle.

A slight twitch of his lip and a faint jolt catch my attention.

"Did you forget about that, at our marriage celebration?" I ask with a quirked brow.

"Yes, I suppose I must have." He rubs the back of his neck, eyes darting away for a moment. "Not to worry, I'll control my protective nature better in your presence going forward."

"Don't. It was admirable and made me hopeful, despite the confusion it caused." The smile I give him stretches up to crinkle the corners of my eyes, and he returns it in kind.

"Well, I suggest getting prepared, I have tailors stopping by shortly. None of your tunics are suitable for *the wife of a historian*," he says in a false, pompous tone, drawing a chuckle from me.

"I'll be ready."

"Wonderful. I look forward to seeing what they stitch together for you." He stands to leave, and I rise to address him.

"May I, um, kiss you on the cheek?" My bravery fails as soon as the words begin to escape.

"You'd want to do that? It's not because of the tunics, is it?" His words are light and wispy as they leave his mouth.

"I've enjoyed our weeks together thus far. Is it... too soon to want it?" I chew my lip, face heating as I feel my remaining courage fade.

"No. In texts I've read, some couples went as far as sexual intercourse within the first twenty-four hours of introductions. N-not that I'm asking for that, but a kiss on the cheek would be wonderful." He rubs the back of his neck once more and sits back down for me.

I close my eyes, breathing deeply, then press my lips against his warm skin. It's slightly rough from the beginnings of his beard growing back, but familiar tingles feel like static in my stomach. Leaning back, I admire the softness that has taken over his face. With his eyes closed, I spend more time than ever appreciating the fullness of his lashes, how welcoming his lips look. Lying my palm against his cheek, I feel empowered as he leans into the sensation.

Reckless even.

Just enough that some long-buried instinct takes control, and I bring my mouth to his.

After a faint inhale, he adjusts to the reality of our situation, kissing me back with tender reservation. I don't know if we're doing it right; who even knows what the correct way to kiss is? But this *feels* right. Before I know what's happening, he presses against me with a bit more force, drawing my lower lip between his teeth and nibbling softly. I pull away, and he whimpers, watching as I run my tongue over the tingling skin.

His eyes drift slowly and examine every detail of my face, expression filled with near child-like wonder. "I-I need to return to my duties. But thank you. I hope you enjoyed that as much as I did." His attention drifts to his lap for a second, coaxing mine down with it. He's sporting an evident erection and, while I'm not yet ready to go that far, the idea isn't as intimidating as before.

Warmth floods through my veins as he flushes, ears turning a vibrant shade of red.

"I apologize, I'll practice better restraint going forward." He makes an effort to adjust himself, but the fitted fabric doesn't allow him to conceal the proof of his arousal.

"Don't be embarrassed. If we were a traditional couple, you would make me please you regularly." As if he needs me to remind him, but I do anyway. Somehow, it proves effective. He offers a slight nod and squeezes my hand before returning to his feet and leaving my room without another word.

Leo stands tall at my side as the tailor takes my measurements, another luxury I would never know without him. The older man from our wedding celebration works with this outfitter. He has given us a wide berth, but Leo is paying close attention to him with judgmental inspection.

"You hold tight to a grudge?" I ask, and the man measuring my waist sputters.

I wince, having forgotten that I need to maintain appearances.

"Yes," Leo responds, regardless. "Nobody tells me how to govern my wife in my home. In fact, the next man to have an issue will be made an example of." His eyes narrow on the middle-aged gentleman working hurriedly to finish his notes.

"You promised you wouldn't threaten to kill anyone..." I squint at him with a small scowl.

"I... did? Right, I recall now." He nods in a way that is not convincing in the slightest.

"Did one kiss wipe your memory?" I tip my head and hear my tailor clear his throat.

"Ah, yes. The kiss. That must be it." He runs a hand through his jet-black hair, mussing it up slightly. "Maybe you can give me another one and see if my memories return." Smiling lazily, he leans against the wall as the man kneeling at my feet finishes his last measurement and hurries away.

"Are you sure this is the place for it, given your reaction before?" I roll my lower lip between my teeth, bringing my gaze to the floor.

Instead of answering, he frames my face with his hands and slots his mouth over mine. The confidence he has this time is bewildering. He leads, and I follow blindly.

Unlike the kiss in my room, he consumes me now. Commanding, claiming, hungry. We're making a scene, but I'm powerless to stop him, to stop me, from letting him take everything he wants. When his lips separate from mine and trail to my jaw, I gasp, falling into his embrace as my knees fail.

"Guides' mercy," he says around a pant, pulling away fully. "I could never get enough of that. What a shame we're not alone." He licks his lips, straightens his ruffled shirt, and pats my hair down.

Breathless and unnaturally warm, I can't muster up a response. Urges and *need* begin to take hold. This must be what true arousal feels like; we're not trained for this. I've wandered into uncharted territory and have no guidelines to help me navigate. I must be more careful in the future. I need to refrain from any kisses like this again until I'm ready to act on these newfound impulses.

"You're spectacular, Darling, just know that this changes nothing. I won't expect anything more from you than you're willing to offer. Never shy away from expressing your disapproval to me. I only ask that you don't lead me on. When you're ready for more, make sure you're *truly* ready." His words sit heavily in the air, a heated proposal.

I nod, understanding exactly what he means. He's ready for more than I am, which, while enticing, terrifies me.

Waiting for the tailor to return, the air around us feels cooler. Perhaps it's a trick of my mind. Whatever this new feeling that has awakened is, I do not appreciate it.

"What has you concerned?" Leo asks.

"I don't know what you're referring to."

"The way you're scrunching your brows tells me everything." He lays his palm against my cheek. "Have I done something to upset you?"

"You can determine my emotions by... watching me?" I stare blindly as his thumb traces small circular patterns on my skin.

"I'm learning. We may not spend an abundant amount of personal time together, but I've taken note of the things you do. In time, I'll be able to read you like the finest tome."

"I thought I upset you, and was contemplating how to proceed regarding these recent developments," I mumble to the floor.

"Don't. We'll never do anything of the sort again until you're prepared for it. I'm aware that things of this nature were not part of your training program or your upbringing. This venture into the realm of love and romance is not something anyone can help us with. But I do know it feels natural. The sensations that your touch and kisses bring to life feel as though they're meant to be. Do be sure to take ample time to prepare for more. I've had years of reading about it to get myself ready." He gently kisses the tip of my nose.

"This all goes against everything I've been taught. You understand that, surely," I retort in a tone that should never come from a woman. Sharp, too direct.

"I am well aware. I have also witnessed the tremendous amount of progress you have made over the past several weeks. Asking questions, fostering your curiosity, laying a solid foundation to gain knowledge that the Guides have proclaimed as off-limits, *especially* for a woman. Yet here you are," he replies unfazed, disregarding my brashness.

"Why do you wish for me to learn so much? You could have easily just taken me as a wife in the New Promise sense. What is the meaning of undoing *years* of training for nothing?" I ask in a hushed tone.

"I have my motivations. You're not yet at a point where I can reveal them to you. I must ensure that you will not endanger anyone when you learn the truth. Please keep an open mind." His voice lowers as he addresses me.

"How would I be endangering anyone? What secrets could you possibly hold? What is behind the door?"

"I'm a historian. My job is not entirely what it seems. I've... learned things not meant for me, but we can't delve into such topics until I know you are ready to hear the truth. And do *not* open the door."

"The truth about wh—"

"Sir, one fitted silk tunic for your wife," the tailor interrupts, handing a parcel to Leo, disregarding my presence altogether.

"Wonderful, thank you for your time. As promised, I have brought silver trinkets from my catacombs for your collection. These are the type of rare buttons you like to affix to clothing, and should be more than suitable for payment." He opens a small pouch, and a collection of flat, shiny fixtures falls into the man's palm.

That is all it takes?

Leo shows no interest in returning to our debate after the tailor leaves us. Truthfully, we have no time. We will be leaving soon and must get ready.

How does one *truly* prepare for their first town meeting?

Stepping out of my room after fastening the tie on my new tunic, I'm greeted by an awestruck Leo. His gaze consumes me. I watch as he licks his lips, followed by the bob of his Adam's Apple as he forces down a hard swallow.

"Guide's mercy, you're radiant. This shade of burgundy complements your porcelain complexion perfectly. May I style your hair, Dearest?" He steps toward me, eyes glimmering as I nod and turn around. Gently, he runs his fingers along my scalp. "Such a perfect auburn. The way your turquoise-colored eyes stand out thanks to it is mesmerizing."

Soft words filled with such admiration flood my body with warmth. My knees threaten to collapse, and I'm overcome with desire. As I turn to face him, I lift onto my toes and pull him to me for a kiss.

His initial surprise confuses me, but once his hands find my waist, I lose myself completely in him. When I moan against his lips, he turns us and presses me into the wall. Of their own volition, my fingers trail down his front, cataloguing the ridges of his abdominal muscles. His palms find my breasts through my tunic, cupping them as he presses into me.

The sensations become too much to bear as he pinches a sensitive nipple. I break the moment, gasping as I pull away.

His chest heaves as he steps back abruptly, gripping his erection through his slacks. "I apologize if I overstepped." His voice is husky, thickly coated with desire. "Please allow me a moment to... relieve myself." Turning on his heel, he retreats to his bedroom before I have a chance to respond.

Tempted to follow, but well aware I'm not ready for him, I have no choice but to wait.

I stroll to the sofa and take a seat, still alight with my own need for release. Would it be inappropriate to find it here? It's not as though Leo will be returning soon, nor will it take me long.

May as well.

Leaning back into the plush cushion, I untie the main sash of my tunic. Sliding my fingers downward, I waste no time circling my aching clit. My hips roll in conjunction as I climb closer to the peak of ecstasy, silently imagining Leo here, his large hands in place of my own.

"Darling, are you—"

I tear my hand away from myself, straightening in my seat, and pull my tunic closed. "Leo, I-I can explain," I sputter as he stands, mouth agape, before me. "I th-thought you would be longer. I know that's not an acceptable excuse. P-please have mercy."

He blinks a few times, then steps toward me, kneeling between my feet. "Would you allow me to assist you? I'd be honored."

"Wh-what?"

"I told you I want to hear all of your sounds. May I earn some now?" He places his hands on my thighs, asking for permission to open them, face soft but filled with evident anticipation.

As I nod, he groans and parts my legs, licking his lips as I'm exposed to him. "Exquisite. Purely exquisite. Do you have any limitations I should be aware of? Is it acceptable for me to use my mouth alongside my hands?" His palms slide up my thighs, closer to my aching core.

"You're welcome to explore me however you wish," I answer on a moan, too aroused to care what that might mean for me.

"If I were to do that, Darling, we would be late for the town meeting. I'll ensure your satisfaction now, as that is my primary concern. My needs will be met when you're ready."

Did he not just tend to his needs?

My questions are lost the instant his mouth makes contact with my inner thigh. As he kisses the tender skin, he slides a finger through my gathered wetness and slips it inside me. Sensations I've never dreamed of come to life as his tongue travels to my clit.

When he inserts a second finger and curls them, I begin to crumble. He works in ways I could never have imagined. Tongue circling with perfect pressure as he presses against a spot inside of me that has my mind on the brink of insanity. Tightness in my core alerts me to my impending release.

Without thinking, I thread my fingers through his hair and thrust my hips, granting myself the final bit of friction required to get me over the edge. As I convulse against him, he groans and presses his face further into me, chasing my moans.

I release my hold, and he pulls back. Interestingly enough, I had anticipated that he would immediately expect reciprocation, despite his earlier statement. The satisfied smirk pulling at his lips has me convinced he actually meant it. There's no indication that he's going to make me please him, which somehow makes me *want* to.

"That was certainly unexpected, but I'm beyond thrilled that you've given me this." He stands, and my eyes trail downward to his sizeable erection, unburdened by slacks, courtesy of his ceremonial tunic. "Soon, when you're ready." He extends a hand and assists me in getting to my feet. My tunic slips open, granting him a full view of my bare breasts, and I revel in the way his eyes flash with appreciation, how his manhood moves on its own at the sight.

"Allow me." He steps up to me and securely ties the golden sash, eyes trailing up my chest and landing on my lips for just a moment before meeting my gaze. "May I kiss you? I can wash my face first, if you'd prefer."

With a soft laugh, I nod, and he leans down, pressing his lips gently against mine. "We must be on our way. Allow me to clean myself up quickly, then we'll depart." He steps into the bathroom and washes his hands and face, then restyles his hair, unbothered by how much I messed it up.

As soon as he's finished, we make haste and head toward the town center.

I had almost forgotten how lifeless and dreary New Promise is. While greenery and moss line the perimeter walls, the rest of the territory is lackluster. Every cobbled street is the same. While I never felt a sense of serenity or found much beauty in the dusty village, my mind seems to have omitted how utterly nondescript and lacking it is.

Except for the town hall, where the Guides and their guards all reside. Unlike the rest of New Promise, they live in luxury. A marble palace with electricity and fresh food. Being a messenger of The Powers Above has its perks, I suppose. They hardly ever marry, but still produce sons to continue their legacies. Concubines or impure unwed women often serve as surrogates for them.

I nearly became one, if it had not been for Leo, nothing more than a vessel for unmarried men who require release, or heirs.

We approach the gilded front door and join the line of fellow citizens waiting to enter. The men converse about various topics, mostly regarding their jobs and goods. Through the gathering crowd, I manage to locate my mother, battered as ever but holding her head high. Pride has always been her driving force. A weaker woman would have run, denounced her marriage, and accepted the public execution. She's an inspiration to many, but also an example to young women of what to expect should they be one of the more unfortunate wives. To me, she's the face of silent betrayal.

The doors open and we file inside, congregating in the large main hall. This room serves many purposes, of which town meetings are the largest.

Still, with approximately one thousand citizens here, it's not quite full.

Shortly after we enter, Raymond approaches us. Leo pulls me closer to his side in preparation, the gesture fills me with familiar excitement. To coincide with his touch, I've also discovered that I quite enjoy his protective actions. No other man in New Promise would dream of threatening another for his wife. Whether or not Leo would act on it is of no importance, the mere insinuation that he *might* is enough to warm my insides.

"Mr. Koeler, has Phoebe been to your liking?" Raymond addresses Leo as if I don't exist.

With a gentle squeeze to my hip where his hand rests, Leo responds, "Quite, Mr. Harding. She's everything I had hoped for and continues to amaze me more with each passing day."

"Just be sure to keep an eye on her. She's always had a tendency to be dramatic. Faking medical episodes to avoid things. You know how crafty women can be, I'm sure." A familiar sneer pulls at his face, causing acid to churn in my stomach.

Tension overtakes my body, pulling at my muscles until I fear I'll fold into myself. Leo's warm hand moves to my back and massages in small circles. The act calms me in a way I don't expect. What would have been a panic attack has been subdued by his simple compassion. I look at him, but his attention is focused solely on Raymond.

"Mr. Harding, I can assure you she's been the perfect wife. Now, if you'll excuse us, I must use the restroom before the meeting begins." He uses the familiar pressure on my lower back to guide me out of the room, ensuring I stay at his side—not behind him.

Once we reach a small, distant meeting room, he guides me to sit on a marble bench inside, closing the sturdy door behind him.

"Are you alright? He's extremely unpleasant, and I must admit it took a great deal of restraint not to strangle him." He kneels in front of me, brushing stray hairs from my face.

A laugh bubbles out of my throat as I dip my head. "If his words were the worst thing ever I had to endure, I'd consider myself fortunate."

"Just know that, if he were to *ever* insult you away from the safety of a crowd, I'd have his entrails pooling at his feet before he knew what was happening." His eyes are clouded over in a way that should probably concern me.

Instead, I'm breathless.

"Would you really?" I ask, running a finger along his jaw.

"For you, I'd do anything."

"Kiss me again?" I plead.

As the last syllable leaves my lips, he claims them with his own. Intense and demanding, he tips my head back, silently requesting *more*. When my mouth opens for him, he slips his tongue inside. Wetness pools between my thighs as he awakens a part of me that has previously lain dormant. Frantic for him, *all of him*, I slip off the bench and into his lap.

"Phoebe," he groans my name, just above a whisper as we settle on the floor. "We mustn't, you're pure. There will be blood. This is not how we should do this."

"But you said anything." I press myself down onto him. Through the thin layers of fabric, I can feel his hardness, his warmth, the proof of how badly he wants me.

"Are you positive you're ready? I would much rather this be special for you, for us." Husky and ragged, his voice fills me with a rush of heat.

My only answer is to untie the front of my tunic, exposing my chest to him. He immediately buries his face in my breasts, hands trailing down my ribs until one settles just above my core. Adjusting my hips, I attempt to gain contact with his fingers, but he moves his hand away. As I attempt to protest, I'm drawn to the motion between us. He unties his tunic and shifts to expose himself to me. Thick and natural, beading with his arousal.

I've only seen him concealed by fabric, but being greeted with the full extent of his manhood is fairly intimidating.

"Oh, my. Please try to be gentle. You're rather large, but I need you in ways I've never known," I beg.

"Don't fret, Darling. This is for you. Say the word, and we can stop if it proves too much. All I ask is that you remain as quiet as possible." Fitting his hands under my thighs, he lifts me with ease and positions us so that I'm lying back on the cool marble floor with only my tunic as a barrier.

Carefully, he aligns himself with my entrance and leans in to claim my mouth. I wince as he presses the very tip into me, the stretch as he slowly dives deeper is sweet torture. Squirming below him, I whimper, and he pauses for a moment, allowing me the chance to breathe. I grasp his shoulders and bite down on his lip as he continues. Inch after inch, I gasp against him, wondering if it will ever end.

No stranger to pain, I push through for the impending reward of pleasure.

One final press of his hips and I've taken all he has to give.

He groans roughly into my mouth before pulling away. "Are you alright?" he asks through a clenched jaw as his control is tested.

I nod in response, brows pinched together as I adjust to the newfound fullness.

"We must be quick. As much as I would love to cherish this moment." He thrusts and I bite back my sound of approval, arching my back from the jolt of painful pleasure. "Powers Above, you're a masterpiece." He trails a hand between my breasts, down my abdomen. "I would enjoy nothing more than to savor our first time, but I fear we're not granted that luxury here."

"I-Oh." My question dies on my tongue as his thumb finds my clit. He traces circles around it, thrusting steadily as my body responds exactly the way he desires. I'm transformed into someone else, free-falling into the moment. A wanton moan rushes out of me and I make no attempt to stop it or let my shame show.

He grows frenzied at the sound, driving into me harder. "That's it." *Thrust* "Fall apart." *Thrust* "Let the whole community hear you." *Thrust*.

Fully at his mercy, I shatter, wailing incoherently as his movements get more forceful.

"Yes, Darling, show them. Let them hear you break for me," he growls, leaning forward to nip at my breasts. His previous concerns about our volume levels have disappeared, taken over by his need to please me.

My core tightens around him further, aching for *more*. As he increases the pace, a second orgasm begins to build deep in my bones. Bodies clashing together, we lose all regard for the rules, not caring where we are. Sounds I've never thought possible erupt from me as he leans back and adjusts my hips so that he can hit an ultra-sensitive spot.

"One more," he pants, pulling back. "Give me one more." He slams back into me, and the last of my restraint breaks.

Forget my training, let The Powers Above judge me for breaking all the rules. I want this.

So I take it.

Moving in time with his thrusts, I mewl and wail to my heart's content, tossing my arms above my head as he claims me here in this "sacred" place. The crazed expression on his face is erotic and helps me topple over the edge. As the powerful orgasm racks my body, he throws his head back, gasping with his own release, filling me with wave after wave of warmth.

Collapsing down onto me, he lets a breathless laugh cross his lips. "I suppose we may have some explaining to do. Hopefully, we're far enough away." A puff of air escapes his nose.

"What happened to being fast and quiet?" I ask, trailing my fingers up and down his arms.

He leans back and pulls out of me, much to my disappointment. "Darling, that was fast, and hopefully to your liking. When we're able to truly enjoy ourselves in the privacy of our dwelling, I'll ensure you never forget the things I make you feel. As for quiet, I simply couldn't resist hearing you. It... was my first time as well, after all. I'm afraid I got carried away in the moment. Forgive me?" He stands and offers me a hand.

"I suppose I can manage that." I smile and let him help me up.

"Fortunately, your tunic conceals the blood. I do apologize for how this happened. Not that I have any regrets aside from the location. Who would I be to deny you in a time of such heated need?" He ties my sash closed and straightens my hair.

"You apologize as though I was not a willing participant," I deadpan.

He chuckles and straightens himself. "Shall we?" He gestures toward the door, and I follow.

I'm starting to believe I'd follow him anywhere.

Leo leads me back to the main hall. Most of the community members have taken their seats on the benches, and the sheer size of our population still amazes me as I scan the room. Our most recent census states that several hundred adult men live here, but seeing them all in one place, most with wives, puts it all into perspective.

We take seats near the front of the crowd, as his status demands, and Leo locks his fingers with mine. I stare down at our connection and am overcome with a serene feeling of peace and acceptance. I'm riddled with nerves, worried people heard us. Based on the lack of reaction, they didn't.

"Please remember your training. This is one of the few times I'll ask this of you." He gently squeezes my hand, but won't look me in the eye.

Right, etiquette.

It's interesting how quickly I've adjusted to the freedoms Leo allows me. Occasionally, I find myself forgetting about New Promise altogether—despite the fact that it's right outside our door. Years of blind belief in our system unraveled in such a short time.

Is my devotion that weak? Would my ancestors disown me?

My pulse quickens for a moment, but then I remind myself that Leo is my husband; his rules are my own now. What I've been taught doesn't matter. Tending to his desires is my duty, and after today, I don't think I'll mind—even if I'll certainly be sore in the morning.

Prime Guide Ogden takes the stand, and the faint murmurs in the room fall to an eerie silence. The same red-headed young guard stands at his side, hands tucked behind his back. I'm not sure how I've never noticed him before our wedding, but now I can't help but watch him. He's handsome, and unlike the rest of the guards, he has a calm, welcoming energy about him. His gaze always seems to find me, which is strangely intriguing.

All seven of the other Guides are in attendance with their guards as well, but they merely sit in the shadows on polished thrones. Prime Guide Ogden taps on the old-world microphone, and feedback echoes off the walls.

"Citizens of New Promise. Welcome to our monthly meeting. This will be a short one, as most women have taken special care to stay true to their husbands." He scans the room, and the air shifts in a chilling way.

He motions to a guard that I had previously not been aware of, and a large door on the side opens. To my surprise, Helena is escorted out, hands secured in front of her by shackles. I stiffen in my seat, and Leo takes immediate notice, squeezing my hand.

"She's the woman you recognized at our wedding. A friend?" he asks quietly. "Don't answer, just squeeze my hand once if I'm correct." I do as he requests, and he grips harder. "I'm terribly sorry, Darling. This will be an especially difficult meeting for you to witness. For your own safety, please remain impassive."

My mind floods with questions.

What does he mean?

Why is she restrained?

What did Prime Guide Ogden mean by staying true to their husbands?

What sort of meeting have I stumbled into?

When she is in the spot designated for her, marked by a red carpet on the floor, Prime Guide Ogden speaks once again. "Mrs. Pierce, the Guides have been informed that you are, in fact, pregnant." He pauses, tapping his fingers against the wooden podium he's standing behind. "Now, for those in the community who are surely confused by what the issue may be, let me enlighten you. Mr. Pierce has not yet undergone the procedure to reverse his mandated sterilization."

Gasps and strings of insults ring out around us. A minor uproar erupts, but the Guides are quick to demand order. Leo sits still next to me, avoiding the confusion on my face.

"Mrs. Pierce has clearly been unfaithful, surely bedding with an unmarried man. Committing such a heinous crime is one thing. Secretly carrying an unapproved child is another. The Guides have no choice but to enforce an equally harsh punishment for your wrongdoing." He snaps his fingers, and her husband, Brock, steps up to the stage.

"Mr. Pierce, would you like the explicit honor of delivering your justice? Or shall you require assistance from a Guide?"

"Don't do it, die alongside her," Leo mutters under his breath.

Die?

"Your graciousness, I would be honored." Brock dips his head and draws *the* button out of his pocket.

Only now do I realize Helena is silently weeping, making no effort to plead her case. She knows that there is no defending yourself to the Guides. Their word is law.

Tears build behind my eyes, and I choke to fight a sob as reality crashes down upon me.

These "meetings" are defenseless trials where women come to die for whatever "transgressions" they've committed.

And Leo did not warn me.

Sensing my upset, he lets go of my hand and wraps his arm around me, burying my face against his chest. I want to protest, to push him away, but his embrace is soothing.

"Wives of New Promise. Let this criminal be an example. Compliance is survival. Mr. Pierce, whenever you're ready." Prime Guide Ogden nods to Brock, who wastes no time.

He holds the button high over his head and presses it without emotion. As if he's not actively murdering his wife and the child she's supposedly carrying. I nearly lurch out of Leo's hold, not that I could do anything to save her. The poison in our punishment capsules is powerful and takes mere seconds to stop the heart. As soon as he releases it, she collapses dead. With the stabbing feeling in my chest, part of my heart dies with her.

Everyone knows the buttons are real, and the poison is considered a kind punishment. I never thought I'd see it in action. I was also unaware of how frequently they are utilized. These are *month-ly* meetings.

Monthly executions.

Tears stream down my face as I turn back to Leo. He rests his chin on top of my head, and I fight to remain silent.

"We'll be leaving in a moment if she was the only one. They'll say a final prayer for Brock and release us."

For Brock?!

The red-haired guard steps off the stage, walking solemnly to lift Helena's lifeless body, and carries her out of the room. I'm fairly certain a tear slides down his cheek despite his rapid blinking to stop it. A strange display of emotion from a man, especially one of such high societal standing.

"Now, let us pray for Mr. Pierce," Prime Guide Ogden begins, breaking the silence that has swallowed the room, "Powers Above, all righteous and all caring, please see that this revered man acquires an acceptable wife in next year's stock. May his future wife be obedient and true to her promises. May her training instill proper values. As it may be."

"As it may be," the room echoes back.

"Until next month, may New Promise remain a sanctuary for those who survived the collapse." As he returns to his throne, the room is dismissed.

Bench by bench, men stand, women follow close behind with damp eyes and sullen expressions.

"This is how they keep women in line. Monthly reminders that, if your husband doesn't do it for something trivial, they'll still have you executed if they see fit," Leo explains. "Just know that if I'm ever put in that position, I won't push the button. Granted, that only means they'll kill me, too."

"They'll kill you if you don't execute me?"

"Yes. The only thing worse than a wife who disobeys is a husband who may dare to care about her." His eyes soften, voice strained.

"But you've stated that I don't have to follow the rules." I peer up at him through my tear-soaked lashes.

"Yes, in our home. However, if you were to break any sort of law, especially in public, they'd have you executed." He rubs my back. "Now let us hurry home. I'm sure you're exhausted."

I nod and follow him out of the hall, too numb to care.

My muscles ache like never before. The bath has helped, and I feel somewhat refreshed as I lift myself out. It's done nothing for the emotional distress, but it was a kind gesture for Leo to draw me one.

Lifelessly dragging myself to the common area, I'm greeted by the sight of him at the stove, finishing up whatever he's managed to make for dinner.

With our garden, it could be anything. The ability to feed ourselves as we see fit and not rely solely on rations is a wonderful amenity.

"Did the bath help, Dearest?" he asks as I amble to the counter.

"No," I reply, toying with a cloth napkin.

"You're thinking about something. Talk to me," he says as though he's oblivious to the happenings from earlier.

"Why did you bring me there?" My voice nearly fails. "W-why did you... h-have intercourse with me and then m-make me watch that?" I push through, brazenly spouting out what's been weighing on my mind.

"Oh." He clears his throat and turns the stove off. "The meetings are mandatory for all men over twenty-one, and all married women... They don't get any easier. Some of the things women are executed for are frivolous and cruel." He plates up fried vegetables that should be appetizing, but my stomach revolts at the thought.

"And my second question?" I double down, raising my chin in dangerous defiance.

"I-I wasn't thinking clearly. Perhaps I was foolish to assume you knew what the meetings entailed. Or maybe it was my desire to please you clouding my judgment."

"PERHAPS?!" I step back, realizing I'm crossing the line into "button" territory of my own.

"I... don't know how else to answer. I understand that the damage I've caused to your trust may be irreparable; for that, I am infinitely sorry." His shoulders slump and the pitiful look on his face squashes some of my anger.

I look at him, nearly shriveled from the self-hatred he feels, and my heart aches. He's only human, we all let our impulses win. It's not as though he forced himself on me. If anything, I pressured him.

Feeling bad about my outburst, I'm overcome with the need to reassure him, so I do.

"No, I apologize for raising my voice. They don't teach us anything about the town meetings. All the years of dutiful training, learning skills to be the perfect wife. Devotion to celibacy for... well, not as many of us as you would think. *All* of that dedication in training, yet they can't even do us the courtesy of telling us the public executions are *real.*"

"I should have warned you. I'm sorry. The thought never crossed my mind. I just wanted to come home, run you a bath, make you nice food, and try cuddling on the couch to see if that would help lift your spirits." His jaw works back and forth, and he stares at the floor.

"I think that cuddling might be nice. But would it be too much of an inconvenience to do it in my bed? I don't wish to eat, merely sleep, which may prove to be an easier feat with your company. Someone to remind me that not all hope is lost." I pass my gaze around the room, landing on everything I can find as I await his response.

"I-uh." With flushed cheeks, he swallows a lump in his throat.

"Please, just accompany me to bed." I place my hand on his chest, enjoying the rapid beating of his heart.

"As you wish, Dearest."

We enter my bedroom, and I make an immediate move to lie down. He's stiff, standing just inside the doorway, hands fidgeting at his sides. With a steadying breath, he steps to the bedside, pulls the covers back and joins me.

"What do we do?" I ask.

"Well, it depends on what you would prefer. N-not referring to intercourse, Guides help me." He groans, pinching the bridge of his nose. "What I mean is, you can either rest your head upon my chest and wrap yourself around me, or face away from me and I'll hold you in my arms. Just know that if you choose the latter, I can not control any natural reactions my body may have."

"I'm quite sore from earlier. You were a bit rough with me. Make no mistake, I enjoyed it, but I'm in no condition to pleasure you again. So, while the second option sounds appealing, it's perhaps not the wisest choice. I would enjoy placing my head on your chest if that's acceptable."

He nods and scoots in closer. As I lay against him, my body releases more of the tension it has been holding. The steady beat of his heart is reassuring and calming. Within minutes of me settling into his side, he's fast asleep.

I take this chance to admire his finer details. The small dimple in his chin, a few freckles on the bridge of his nose. His lower lip has a faint scar I can just make out from this angle. Sleeping like this, it's hard to picture him threatening to gut my father earlier.

He's definitely a peculiar man, but I wholeheartedly believe that he would rather die than be the one to execute me. Hopefully, we'll never have to test that claim.

Cuddling is amazing. Why did we ever stop doing this? Why did we ever stop loving one another? Even now, as I lie here with Leo's arms around me, I feel a sense of security beyond my comprehension. He rolled toward me in the night, and I've lain here enveloped in his warmth and crisp, fresh scent, since.

Despite my initial upset, I don't believe he intentionally deceived me yesterday. He likely knows just a slight amount more than I do regarding how New Promise operates. In the short time that I've been his wife, he's shown me things I thought were merely fables. The least I can do is trust that he had no ill intent.

The things he made me feel on that polished marble floor definitely didn't give me the impression of malice. Thinking of them now, as I listen to his breathing, my chest feels as though it's swelling with fuzzy sensations. I'm overcome with the urge to *feel* him again, pushing my body to new, excruciatingly pleasurable limits.

Would he mind if I touched him like this? Is it acceptable to initiate an intimate encounter while he's peacefully sleeping?

Holding my breath, I shy away from his face as my touch travels slowly down his abdomen, landing on his half-erect manhood. Gently gripping, I admire how he grows harder in my hand. As I begin to stroke him, he stirs.

"Dearest, what—" A ragged moan interrupts his words as I gently slip the tip of my finger under his foreskin and circle the swollen head nestled within.

"I'm not upset with you any longer. I-I would like to be intimate with you again," I admit, whispering against his chest.

"You, uh, okay." He blinks and rolls onto his back. "How do you want to do this?" I pause at the question, and he tenses. "Did I do something wrong?" he asks, voice rough from sleep and breathy.

"No, it's just that yesterday you took charge and left me no room to think about logistics. I was not trained to have choices or make decisions about how I should pleasure you." I sit up and untie my sleep gown.

His gaze lingers on my hardened nipples, and he licks his lips. "I uh, want you to get on top of me and pleasure both of us. Let me watch your breasts as you move."

A sudden bout of blush heats my cheeks, and I flush bright red down to my chest. I am unprepared for this scenario, but I ache to feel him inside of me again. Fighting the awkwardness, I climb over him and shed my sleep gown altogether. Hungrily, his hands grab hold of my breasts and begin to knead. As I line myself up with him, he pauses—anticipation lights his features, as if this is our first time all over again.

I'm fairly certain he's holding his breath.

Sinking slowly onto his length, I brace myself on his chest, nails digging into his skin as I continue. He feels bigger today, not in length, but in girth. I don't remember the stretch being quite so blissfully agonizing yesterday. Still, I continue until every bit of him is securely inside of me... which also feels a bit different.

The dreamy look on his face as I rise and lower myself is encouraging. Despite how awkward I feel, he's enjoying himself. Quickening my pace, I toss my head back and mutter his name on a gasp, causing a groan to break free from his throat. He tilts his hips, adjusting my angle, and I writhe from the sensation.

As I continue to work us both closer to the edge, he moans in approval and plays with my tender nipples.

Trailing one hand to my clitoris, he begins tracing firm circles until I quiver. "You're the most spectacular woman in all of New Promise. Look at you pleasuring both of us. I'm so fortunate to have you." He pulls me down and claims my mouth, thrusting as I stop moving. "Are you close to your climax, Dearest? I don't want to find my release without you," he grits out as we separate.

"I am." I breathe against his lips, trembling as my inner walls clench.

"Let me help you." He nibbles at my neck and thrusts roughly several times as I scream.

When my core tightens and I erupt, he joins eagerly, whimpering my name as he loses himself.

"This was... not what I expected." I pant. "But I enjoyed it just the same." Smiling down at him, I find joy in the blissful smile he's sporting.

When I move to get off him, a commotion in the kitchen startles me.

"Is someone here?" I ask, keeping my voice hushed, "Who would possibly be here?"

"I'll go check, stay out of sight." He moves me to the side, pulls his sleep pants on, exiting the room in a flash.

Foolishly, I follow. Call it poor survival instinct, or morbid curiosity.

If there's danger, I don't want him facing it alone. I'm not sure what good I'll be in fending off an attacker, but there's strength in numbers, and I'd rather be executed than let him be harmed.

I hear him engaging in a quiet conversation as I grow closer.

The sight awaiting me as I reach the end of the hall makes my blood run cold.

All the minor inconsistencies make perfect sense now. As I gasp, they turn to face me, matching eyes wide and panicked. Overcome with a sense of betrayal, I sprint back to the safety of my room and hurry to lock the deadbolt.

"Darling, please. We can explain." Leo's voice sounds from the other side of the door, at least, I can only assume that's his name.

"Please, Dearest. We... wanted to tell you soon. Then the intimacy happened, and it all got mixed up," the other one says. The one who was just lying in bed with me, taking my pleasure for his own.

Breathing rapidly, I strain, trying to make sense of what I've just witnessed. Are there more? Are they real? Would they deceive me more if I asked?

"Please?" they beg in unison, and it's too much.

My stomach lurches, threatening to expel any contents it may still hold. My vision goes spotty as my heart hammers in my chest. How am I supposed to stop the panic attack when the only person who helps is the cause?

I attempt to reach my bed but collapse just before I'm able to make it.

"I tried to tell you she'd react poorly the longer we continued this charade."

"I know, but I wanted to be sure it was safe to share our secret with her."

Their voices are nearly identical, but hearing them together, I find slight tonal differences I have otherwise missed.

"You shouldn't have been intimate with her yet. It's all overly complicated now," the tender one who calls me 'Dearest' with a slightly gentler undertone declares.

"Oh, and what do you have to say about this morning? Also, if I'm not mistaken, *you* were the first to kiss her," the more serious one, Mr. 'Darling', fires back.

"She asked to kiss my cheek, and then *she* kissed *me*. It's not the same as claiming her loudly at town hall while the *entire* community is there to bear witness," 'Dearest' retorts.

"She asked me nicely, I couldn't deny her," 'Darling' responds.

Wait.

If I locked myself in my room, why do they sound so close? Why am I in a bed?

I lean up on my elbows and pry my eyes open. I'm in my bed, my door removed from its hinges. Both men are present, arguing among themselves in the sitting chairs. The instant they notice I'm conscious, they stand and come to either side of me.

"What are you?" I ask, brows scrunched with a grimace on my face. Despite my unease and confusion, I do not flinch.

"We're what is known as identical twins, Phoebe," 'Darling' says, voice softer than usual.

"But how? Families aren't allowed more than one child." My head spins, throwing my balance off. I drop from my elbows and sink into the pillows.

"Well, we've spent the last twenty-six years pretending we're the same person. It's been a challenge, and I was always a bit more awkward than Leo, so he often was the one who went out and did things. I'm a homebody, so I don't mind," 'Dearest' explains.

I tilt my head toward him and huff out a breath. "So, what's your name then? I can't call you both Leo, and I can't exactly *avoid* you while living under the same roof."

"Well, Leo is technically your husband, so—"

"No, Max. That's *not* the agreement, and you know it," Leo interrupts with an irritated edge to his voice.

"It's true, though. All your life, you've sacrificed for me. I-uh, well, Phoebe should have a say," Max offers as if I have the faintest idea of what they're talking about.

I shake my head and sit up to address them. They're eerily similar, and I feel a sense of confusion and awe as I look between them.

"I have questions. Will you answer them truthfully?" I ask.

"Yes," they confirm simultaneously.

"You're the only two, correct? No more surprise identical men?"

"We are," Leo answers to my left.

"And your name is Max?" I look to my right.

"Yes, we're technically Leonidas and Maximus. Our parents had a love for ancient names." He shrugs.

"I... wow. I thought I was crazy. The community always spoke of Leo as a strange man, one who seemed to act completely different each time you met him. The mysterious historian, destined to live in seclusion for all his days. Too strange to integrate."

"We only look identical. Our personalities are fairly different," Leo explains with a soft laugh. "Max stopped going to the community a few years ago. We almost got discovered, and that would be deadly."

"Deadly?" I sit up straighter and look between them, noting their worried expressions. Matching forehead creases from furrowed brows, similar scowls aside from that telltale scar on Max's lip. The one I have purposefully ignored and convinced myself just "faded" depending on the day.

"Yes. It's why we didn't tell you at first. We had to be sure you were the right woman. If we told you too soon and you tried to run, we'd have no choice but to press the button... if we didn't and the community found out, they'd banish both of us." Leo stares at the bedsheets as he explains.

"So, you've been playing tricks on me? Swapping back and forth as you see fit. Was it a competition to see who could win my heart? What was the grand scheme?" I clutch at my chest as my breathing fluctuates.

"Easy, Dar-uh Phoebe. We were not accounting for how quickly our relationship would progress. We were also not entirely positive you would find both of us appealing. If you favored one of us over the other, then the least desired one of us would have stayed away. But you were genuinely interested in each of us." Leo moves to reach for my hand, but pulls back after brief consideration.

"I was sure it would be me who would be stuck in this room forever. But the first time I met you, and you asked me to cuddle on the couch, I got flustered and had to dart off so Leo could take the situation out of my hands. I-I wasn't expecting you to like me, but when you did, I was conflicted," Max says to the floor, voice trembling.

"You were with me at the meeting yesterday." I look to Leo in question.

He nods, licking his lips. "I was also the one with you as the tailor was measuring you for your tunic," he confirms.

"So then, Max, it was you this morning?"

He flushes and nods. "It was also me in the hall-way. I... let my urges take hold a bit more than I should have, my apologies," he murmurs.

"What is the point of all of this? Why marry a woman just to lie to her and hope she doesn't run away?"

"We were hoping you'd be our wife," they answer at the same time.

"Excuse me?!" I jolt. "Were my wishes taken into consideration at any point while you were con-cocting this ludicrous plan?" They freeze, faces blanching. "Precisely. For men who claim to be different, you've surely only thought of yourselves in all of this." I rise from the bed and storm out of the room. "Do not follow me!" I yell, making my way toward the entry hatch.

Leo could press the button for this; I wouldn't blame him. I saw the fear in his eyes as I lashed out.

Serves them right, inconsiderate *men.*

I stomp up the steps, ensuring I'm heard, and head to the garden. It's overcast, and the air is damp. A rare storm is rolling in.

Of course.

I collapse and let my tears fall, soaking into the verdant earth below my knees. Heaving sobs rack my body as I take what may be my last breaths—if they have so little faith in me, they believe I went to the Guides. Acid burns my throat as I bite back the bitter taste of their selfishness.

How am I supposed to be a wife to both of them?

I toss my head back, staring at the cloud-filled sky, and wail as the raindrops begin to fall, hands clenched into tight fists. For what must be hours, I sit and cry endless tears of rage and confusion until I begin to shiver as the night settles in.

To their credit, they have not come in search of me. Yet, I still live.

Stepping back inside feels like an impossible task. Could I survive out here for a night if the rain stops? Maybe two? How long until I'm able to look at them, let alone consider forgiveness?

Squash vines wrap around the garden bed, and I pull a few, weaving them together in an intricate pattern, calming my mind. Focusing on my task, the nighttime chill is forgotten. My hands may be numb, but they're determined to finish my small basket.

I'm not sure how long it takes, but the sun has officially left me with a mere sliver of light. The hens have quieted for the evening, settling down to sleep, and I yawn in agreement. I've been out here all day, wallowing in my misery. At this point, I can no longer pretend that sleeping outside is an option.

Bracing myself for what's to come, I stand and open the hatch. Staring into the darkness that once felt like home, I give myself a moment before taking the first step, the tricky landing that Leo still hasn't had fixed. I tread carefully, keeping quiet as I reach the ground floor. Only now do I realize how cold I am. Shivers make my body tremble uncontrollably, my fingers burn from being chilled to the bone. Nose running from the warmth, I scurry to my bedroom and quickly hide under the covers.

It is no use, I'm drenched and must be near hypothermia. As I struggle to drag myself out of bed, I do the first thing I can think of and look for them. They didn't execute me, surely they will help me in a time of need. Right?

They are not in the main room, which tells me they're in Leo's bedroom or study. Dragging my feet, I sniffle and make it to Leo's door, opening it without announcing myself.

Fresh tears try to build as I find them here, sitting with glasses of whisky, disheveled and clearly upset. I can't vocalize my problems, so I dart my attention back and forth, whimpering to get their attention. I'm not sure that I do, but I think I hear them say something just as my vision fades to black.

Rustling to my left catches my attention as I stir. Rubbing my temples, I sit forward and stretch. And then my mind readjusts. I'm warm, comfortable, safe. They took care of me, even after I lashed out. Both of them.

I'm unsure of where I am; this bed differs from the others. Bigger. Softer.

Only one of them is still present. Judging by the slight scowl on his face and how he's holding his shoulders, this is Leo. Leaning forward onto his knees, staring blankly at the wall, he hasn't noticed I'm awake.

"Where is Max?" I ask, voice rough, and his attention snaps to me before he stands.

How long was I out this time?

"He had to use the restroom. He shall return momentarily." Tentatively, he sits on the edge of the bed. "Are you still angry? Rightfully so. Just know that our deceit was not intended to cause harm. We planned to tell you, eventually."

"I-I'm not angry anymore, mostly confused. How did I get into this room?"

"This, Darling, is our room. The bed is large, intended to sleep several people comfortably. It has been off-limits to you until now because we would take turns and hide out in here while the other was spending his time with you. Which is why you could hear movement occasionally." A soft expression crosses his face.

"This is what lies beyond the locked door? You planned for me to share this room, this bed, with both of you?" I rub my forehead, leaning back against the headboard.

"It was our hope. Our parents were in love, and died for it. Despite that fact, Max and I have wanted nothing more than to feel the same things we grew up witnessing."

"He's telling the truth," Max says as he enters the room. "Clearly, I could not try to find my own wife, as I do not officially exist." He rolls his lips together and sits opposite Leo on the bed. "Our goal was to divide our time with you and eventually reveal the truth *before* things became too involved."

"But I sabotaged the plan?" I ask, overcome with gnawing guilt.

"No, you merely expedited the process. Whether you feel comfortable lying with both of us is up to you. We will not force you. Just know you're still my wife, and as such I will ensure you're fed and housed... and cared for when you collapse." Leo speaks to me directly, firm hand laying atop my foot through the blankets.

"You won't force me? Even if I do not want you?" I swallow hard, looking between them.

"We would never be so cruel. Just, please don't expose us to the Guides. I do not wish to die," Max pleads from my other side.

"May I have time to properly ponder my decision? Prior to the town meeting, I had never been intimate with a man. Now you're requesting that I be intimate with two?" I inhale deeply as my heart hammers. The exact reason for it escapes me—dread, uncertainty, a strange bit of excitement. I feel deranged and wrong.

"Darling, forgive my frankness, but you've already been intimate with both of us," Leo says gently, but that does little for my peace of mind.

"And you've been spending time with each of us separately. The only distinct difference will be that one of us won't have to live in the shadows at all times," Max adds, voice soft and light.

"Alas, I may enjoy a warm meal again." Leo groans.

"Wh-what?" I jolt, eyes piercing him.

"You see, we had to decide how best to manage our time. Since you had taken a liking to visiting me in the study, and Max is the better cook, we decided that meal times would be best suited to him, and the down times would be my chance to enjoy your company," he explains, holding my gaze as he massages my foot through the plush fabric.

My mind urges me to pull away from his touch, but the fraction of comfort it brings cannot be explained. Therefore, I don't protest. Instead, I sit for several moments, mulling over the information they've thrust upon me.

While their scheme was cruel, *they* never have been. They warmed after I endangered myself, and have not so much as scolded me for acting in such a foolish way. Still, I'm unsure of how I feel.

Used.

Wanted.

Manipulated.

Foolish.

Cared for.

I swallow hard and look between them. Two identical sets of deep brown, caring eyes stare solemnly back at me.

Leo, intently watching my every move, analyzing and cataloging the emotions rushing across my face. His touch steady, grounding, a welcome tether to reality.

Max, hands folded in his lap, takes in the way my breathing fluctuates. Eagerness to reach out and comfort me dances across his down-turned expression.

"I'm no fool," I spit in challenge, latching onto anger and hurt amidst the web of emotions in my body.

"We know," they respond in unison, voices meek.

"Then why have you made one of me? Leading me to believe you're genuine whilst trading me back and forth like the impure, unmarried women of New Promise? Am I not worthy of your honesty?"

They look to one another, then to me.

"Have we not explained our reasoning?" Leo asks flatly, a hint of irritation in his tone.

"What he means is, it had nothing to do with your worthiness as a wife. We have lived a forbidden life and must take necessary precautions, Phoebe," Max offers, voice more assertive than I've witnessed, while somehow remaining soothing.

"You pass me around like I'm an object while telling me I'm special." Tears begin to stream down my face. Buried emotions I've never allowed to surface pool just below my skin, eager to break free. "Foolishly, I had believed I was starting to feel love for you!"

They both pale at my outburst.

"H-how am I to know which one of you I was gaining feelings for?" Pulling my knees to my chest, I curl into my own safety. "Cruelty is not merely physical. Parts of me ache that my father could never touch. Do you understand?"

Their faces fall as I continue, allowing me to relieve the built-up frustrations in a way the garden could not.

"I-I..." Words fail, my mind goes numb.

Looking around the room, I take notice of details I hadn't bothered to see. The open closet has an empty section where only my bridal tunic hangs. Three sitting chairs are tucked into a far corner. Against the back wall is another vanity table, my name etched beautifully into the edge. The sight gives me pause.

"How long has this room been prepared?" I ask around my tears.

"Since I first laid eyes on you months ago," Leo responds faintly.

"He came home from the community and told me he saw our future wife," Max speaks up, voice hushed and pained.

"You-you knew for *months*?" I shake my head. "Then why did you wait so long to claim me? I could have escaped so many lashings." Fresh tears and a new batch of emotions bubble out of me. I tremble as the worst months of my life flood back into my memory. The pain and upset throw me into a heightened panic.

As the air around me becomes nearly solid, I struggle to inhale. Sweat coats my body as I tightly grip the blankets, attempting to anchor myself to the present.

"Phoebe," Max calls out from my right.

"Do try and breathe for us," Leo attempts to calm me.

I watch through blurry eyes as they share a look. With quickly exchanged nods, they move to either side of me on the bed. Max, pulling me against his chest, murmurs soft, calming words into my ear. Leo curls around me from behind, running his fingers along my scalp.

Surrounded by them, the rest of the world ceases to exist. In their shared embrace, I feel more whole than I've ever imagined.

"The Guides would not allow me to marry you at first. They view you as lesser, unworthy of mothering a future historian because of your father. The fight for your hand was torturous," Leo whispers against my hair.

"We shared many a night plotting to steal you away, regardless of what that may have meant. Our only focus was you." Max swipes hot tears from my face.

In a flurry, desperate to latch onto something tangible, I grip the front of his shirt and kiss him without reservation. He grunts at first, before locking his hand behind my neck and leaning into it. Leo trails his fingers down my arm, pressing his lips to my shoulder.

As I pull away from Max with a gasp, Leo is there, taking what he wants from me. I turn toward him, deepening our connection as Max brings his mouth to my neck, peppering soft kisses along my collarbone.

"As much as we would love to have you again, I'm afraid now is not an appropriate time," Leo breathes out as he breaks our contact.

I whine as the throbbing between my thighs protests.

"He's correct, Dearest. There are many things we need to discuss. Things we should have made you aware of before we got this far," Max says softly against the heated skin of my chest. "You are delectable, and I must avoid the temptation." He groans and rolls away from me, hardness straining against his trousers.

"Allow us the opportunity to be fully honest with you, and then you can have us both at once if you desire. Do take the time to be angry with us if you need," Leo tells me as he, too, rolls away.

"Speak your truths now, then," I demand.

They chuckle and stand from the bed.

"Darling, it's dinner time. May we eat first? I'm quite eager for that hot meal I mentioned." Leo offers a soft smile and turns to excuse himself.

"Max," I pout. "May I please you?" I stare down at his erection.

"Guides give me strength." He blows out a harsh breath. "Let us make up for our wrong-doings, please? Leo is also severely deprived of hot food. He has been a miserable bastard for weeks." He smiles playfully.

"Well, we'd best get to work then, I suppose." I take one final, long breath and slide out of the bed.

By the time I reach the kitchen, Leo is already sitting at the table, plates and forks laid out for the three of us. Seeing my spot in the middle makes my stomach feel as though it is tumbling.

Max and I fall into a comfortable rhythm. Weeks of preparing meals together have made us in tune while we cook. Leo watches intently with an adoring smile spread across his face. The warmth in his gaze is endearing.

My overwhelming emotions dissipate more and more as the minutes pass. Our familiar ease settles in as I look at each of them. Their tension is still evident, but I find myself almost humored by the way I reacted.

One roast hen and sautéed vegetable medley later, I take my seat at the table while Max brings our final dishes over.

I admire his knife skills, yet again, as he carves portions out for the three of us. Leo's face lights up with the first bite, sighing in contentment as he chews. Such a sight warms my insides, knowing I'm responsible for his enjoyment. Or, at least partially so.

"Every meal you two have prepared has smelled divine. While eating them cold hours after the fact has been acceptable, this—" He takes another bite and groans. "—this is exceptional."

We eat in silence for some time, forks clinking against the ceramic. As I savor the meal, watching them enjoy themselves, I long for more of this.

I bury my personal feelings and consider theirs. Living in fear is not a foreign concept to me. Thinking back to all the times I nearly withered from Raymond's heavy-handed discipline, I realize their situation, while not physically damaging, is eerily similar. They were forced to live a life that sheltered them and left them no chance to social-ize outside of one another. In no world can I fault them for simply trying to survive.

"I..." Pushing my food around the plate before me, I take a moment to plan my statement. "I am willing to forgive you both for what you've done. I understand that we all do what we must to survive in this world. While I was initially upset and felt as though you were being cruel, I understand how difficult it must have been for you."

"The hardest part has been keeping ourselves from you," Max responds. "I can't speak for Leo, but I wanted to spend all of my free moments with you these past several weeks. Feeling like an illicit affair, coordinating around your time with him proved hurtful."

"I concur. Hearing the two of you make memories whilst cooking wonderful meals made me ache to join you. And then there's the matter of hearing you together in the bedroom." He looks me in the eye, only veering to Max for a moment.

"Were you... upset by it?" I ask, voice small.

"Only because I could not partake."

I drop my fork as his words settle in. "You mean it then. Both of you would like to—"

"To love you, Darling. We want all of what you're willing to provide," he announces.

"If you do not wish to be intimate with us simultaneously, we will not impose." Max takes my hand and squeezes gently. "But we would enjoy spending *all* of our time together as the three of us. Perhaps cuddling on the sofa tonight would be a nice introduction?" His crooked smirk and pink-stained cheeks are magnetic, pulling at my aching soul.

"I'll find a nice story to read while we sit and allow our meals to settle." Leo decides for me, then stands and gathers our plates, taking them to the sink before veering off to his study.

Max and I make our way to the sofa and await his return. We sit next to each other, as if we've never touched before, as if I'm not still tender from our intimacy. His shoulders are stiff, breathing shallow.

As Leo enters the room, Max relaxes in his presence. "Brother, please ease yourself, she's here because she wishes to be," Leo says, taking a seat on my opposite side. "How would you like to sit, Darling?" He leans back, legs uncrossed, a familiar invitation to climb onto him.

I look to Max, unsure of how he'll respond. As I sit against Leo's chest, Max slides next to him, pulling my legs into his lap. He massages my feet and legs as Leo reads us a grand tale of mythical beasts and wondrous adventures.

Aching in my chest subsides as we sit in peaceful companionship.

Perhaps this won't be a terrible arrangement. Unorthodox? Surely, but this could prove enjoyable. Where Leo is a grounding force of comfort, Max is warm and offers security in my harshest moments.

Wherever this may go, I'm not sure, but it starts now.

True to their word, Max and Leo allowed me to sleep in my bed last night. Detrimental, that's what it was. Free time to be alone with my thoughts is dangerous. I still have many questions, and the quest for answers only proves to upset me.

Emerging from my room, I amble to the kitchen, feeling as though I did not sleep a second. Both of them are already awake, sipping tea as they sit at the table. The sight feels right. They must do this frequently. Or, they did before me.

"Good morning, Dearest. Care to assist me with breakfast duties? Then the three of us can tend to the garden. I've propagated more of the squash you enjoy." Max stands, tea in hand, and moves to the storage box.

"Do you always share your mornings?"

"We share nearly everything, Darling," Leo answers from his seat at the table. His meaning is unmistakable.

"Are you aware that the different nicknames were one of my first indicators that something was off with you?" I ask around the tingles left from his statement.

"Is it uncommon for one to call his wife by a nickname? Our parents did it." Max tilts his head, causing his unstyled black locks to shift over his brow.

They're much more relaxed today, and I quite like it.

I shake my head and answer him, "No, men call their women by name. Your parents were an oddity. And your inconsistent names struck me as even more strange. The men of New Promise are cruel, even the 'nice' ones. This is why I still fear upsetting you." I look to Leo, who is wearing a tense expression. "Both of you," I whisper to the floor.

"We're not those men. We were raised in a home built on love, by parents who detested New Promise," Max mutters as he turns toward me, eggs and vegetables in hand.

I straighten, eyes wide. "Your parents detested New Promise? But the Guides are our saviors. They maintain the peace and ensure The Powers Above are satisfied."

"The guides from generations ago may have been, but who can truly be sure what their intentions were," Leo says, stepping to my side. "Our parents were seen as heretics and, once I was twenty-one and old enough to take our father's position, they were sent to the wastes—banished to death for thinking freely."

"They, they do that? I thought they just execute people?" I gasp, gripping the countertop.

"When a man steps out of line, refusing to murder his wife, they punish him, too. Instead of executing them humanely, they choose torture in the form of sending them into the uninhabitable wasteland beyond our barrier walls." Leo swallows hard. "Our parents went to that meeting knowing exactly what would happen, hand in hand, with no fear. Their love for one another made them brave."

"Or careless." The words leave my mouth before I can stop them.

"I would be careless and walk into death ten times over if it meant I could enjoy a love like the one they shared," Max proclaims as he cracks eggs into a bowl.

"As would I. You haven't witnessed the joy that comes with loving and being loved in return." Leo rubs my back for a moment before withdrawing his hand. "My apologies."

"Your touch does not offend me. I... I want to attempt loving both of you, but what if it means death?"

"I would face death for your love any day," Leo replies, returning his hand to my back.

"And I would gladly walk by your side to our mutual demise," Max turns and speaks directly to me, eyes locking with mine.

"Someday I hope that I'll feel the same. Though I do not wish to die." I chew my lip. "May I ask a favor?"

"Anything," they chant at the same time.

A small giggle rushes out of me, finding their synchronicity endearing. "May we start with sharing the large bedroom? The mattress is much more comfortable than the one in my current room. I also would like the opportunity to spend more time cuddling with both of you at once." I avoid their gazes, but catch the knowing expression on Leo's face as I dart my eyes to the floor.

"Darling." He tucks a finger under my chin, lifting my face. "Whatever reason you must give is enough for us. Our room is yours as well."

I swallow harshly and nod in his hold, knees weak, stomach on fire.

"We can move your belongings after breakfast. For now, would you like to whisk these eggs for me, Dearest?" Max hands me the bowl, and I silently get to work.

Leo assists as much as we allow, but he truly is not handy in the kitchen.

Max is much more relaxed with him around, joking and poking fun at his brother. It feels so natural. Such a shame that more women don't live a life like this.

We finish making breakfast and clean up, then carry on to the garden. Our little plot between the border walls has grown significantly over the last few weeks. Max has cleared additional tillable land and laid out more area to plant some of my favorite vegetables. Carrots and squash are delicious; their sweet and earthy flavors make them ideal for a variety of dishes. We've also increased the amount of fresh herbs, ensuring I have an adequate supply of chives to keep me happy.

Leo also bartered with a farmer to add two new hens to our flock. They've integrated well and already love me. We all smile and laugh as we pull weeds and ensure the crops have enough water to thrive.

As we re-enter the house, I yawn and stretch, exhausted from the lack of rest and emotional overload from yesterday.

"Would you like a bath and a nap, Darling?" Leo rubs my back.

"I think that would be quite nice, thank you."

"I shall start the water for you," Max makes haste to the bathroom.

I chuckle as he disappears down the hall. "He's eager to please me, isn't he?"

"Quite. We both are, to be clear." Leo moves my hair to the side, running his finger through my knots. "Go on and get settled in the water. I shall bring a tunic for you, so long as you're comfortable with that."

My thoughts freeze for a moment.

Am I okay with him seeing me in the bath?

While I have been intimate with each of them, this somehow feels more vulnerable. I ponder for only a second before making my decision.

"That would be acceptable." I smile and saunter toward the bathroom with him following close behind.

As I enter, Max is still here testing the water as it pours from the faucet. Leo leaves us and heads to my room next door.

"I, uh, don't know how hot you like it. Leo is the only one who has drawn you a bath." Max flushes. "My apologies if it's not satisfactory. I added some herbs and oils that I pressed."

I dip my hand in the water and swirl it around before standing up on my toes, kissing him on the cheek. "It's perfect. Thank you."

He holds me, staring into my eyes for a moment. The air in the room is misty from the heat of the water, wrapping around us in a fantastical manner, smelling of mint and lavender. Drawn to his essence as the world fades away, I nearly lose myself in the beauty of this moment.

"May I assist you with this?" Gripping the tie on my tunic, his voice ghosts over the skin of my neck.

"I would appreciate it." I step away slightly, allowing him easier access to the cords.

Do I *need* his assistance? No. But I'm feeling rather adventurous, and also enjoy fostering his bravery. I lift my arms and lay my hands on his shoulders as he pulls the ends of my sash. When the front slips open, his eyes find my bare chest for a split second before jumping to my face.

"Allow me," Leo's voice breaks through the tension in the room. He places my clean change of clothes on the bench and steps behind me, slipping the arms of my tunic down. As it hits the floor, I become abundantly aware that I'm *fully* exposed to both of them.

Should I feel ashamed?

The rules of New Promise tell me that no man other than my husband shall ever see me in the nude.

But Max isn't just *any* other man, and judging by the way both of them have stepped to my front and begun admiring me, my husband doesn't mind.

"Powers Above," Leo breathes out.

"I-um. You're—" Max gulps.

"Would you like to sit with me while I bathe?" I ask, sure of their answers.

"Please," their strained voices echo through the room.

"Are you positive? There are no pressing matters that require your immediate attention?" Smiling coyly, I sink into the tub, humming in approval as I settle. "This is wonderful, Max. Thank you."

"You're welcome, Dearest." He groans as I cup water in my hand and drip it over my breasts.

They're each wearing casual tunics. The thin fabrics offer minimal concealment for their erections. Zings of arousal dart through my body as I drink them in. I'm not ready for the two of them, but knowing their attraction is so strong surely makes me *feel* as though I could be.

"Leo, would you mind washing my hair? You quite like running your hands through it."

"As you wish, Darling." He crosses the room to stand at the front of the tub. "Would you be so kind as to wet your it for me?"

I do as he asks, lying back to submerge my head. As I lift it back out of the water, he's there with soaped hands. I lift a leg above the surface as he scrubs my head, directing my attention to Max. "Would you be a dear and wash my feet? I quite enjoy the massages you give."

"Your wish is my pleasure to fulfill." He steps to the end of the tub and gathers soap in his hands.

Together, they pamper me in ways I never would have imagined. Strong hands knead muscles I hadn't previously realized were sore. They maintain respectful gazes while washing my body, though I can feel their restraint pulling taut as they each glide a soapy hand over my breasts. My own will is tested when Max slips a hand into the water and along my inner thigh. I nearly gasp when Leo's fingers graze my nether regions as he washes my stomach. Surely they're painfully erect, yet neither of them presses further, allowing me to enjoy the sensations free of expectations.

As I lean forward to drain the water, the air shifts. Leo goes eerily silent behind me.

He doesn't have to say a word.

The expression on Max's face tells me they're exchanging looks of disgust.

I sit still, awaiting words that may break my spirit. Staring at my lap, I tremble as the silence between us grows louder. That is, until I feel fingertips lightly tracing the marks on my back.

"Phoebe," Leo whispers, hurt lacing my name as it leaves his lips. "What—"

"Surely you can draw an accurate conclusion," I snap, cutting him off. "I apologize if my appearance repulses you."

"What?!" Max exclaims, lurching his head back. "Why would we be repulsed?"

"You're not looking at what he sees, Max. I'm disfigured, unattractive, ruined." My chest tightens as familiar dread sets in. "The two of you have made me feel so adored that I had forgotten about the scars. It hadn't crossed my mind that neither of you has seen me fully nude until right now."

"Your father?" Leo asks, a faint edge cutting through his words. "I apologize for not seeing them before."

"Who else?" I move to grab the replacement tunic, but I'm stopped by two sets of strong hands. "Please allow me to cover them. I apologize for the discomfort that looking at them must cause." My brows knit together as I beg them for understanding.

"You're not repulsive, I'm just so terribly sorry we couldn't do anything sooner." Max wraps me in a tight embrace.

"I may be able to procure ingredients for a salve that could help them fade, if you would like. Know that they do not make you less perfect to me." Leo continues to trace the deep gash scars lining my lower back, gently kissing along them. "You could never repulse either of us, Darling."

"He speaks the truth," Max confirms, brushing wet hair from my face. "Let's get you to bed."

"Can—"

"Yes," they both answer, following me out of the bathroom into *our* room.

A quick nap would be amazing. I secretly hope they'll stay with me through all of it. I may have only done it a time or two, but I've found that I sleep better when I'm not alone.

I had feared the worst when I heard I would marry—had assumed my father ruined me for any potential husband.

How fortunate I am to be in the presence of the last two good men alive.

Waking up between my men has become the best part of my mornings. As I lie here, eyes closed and curled into Max, Leo's breath puffs against my shoulder. I must admit this is wonderful. Three nights now we've been sharing our room, and our days as a whole. We've not been intimate, and they maintain a respectful distance through most of the day—cuddling excluded. We've naturally fallen into a lovely pattern.

Warm and secure in their arms, I nuzzle closer into Max, slipping his sleep tunic open slightly. I place my cheek upon the skin of his chest, and he stirs.

"One moment, Dearest." He leans away, shifting just enough to work his upper body free of the fabric.

I trace the line of his collarbone, down between his defined pectorals. His abdominal muscles flex as I trail lower, outlining the ridges as I did when we kissed in the hallway.

"Darling," Leo's voice rumbles in his chest, pressed against my back. "You're going to make him burst. Please have mercy."

I tilt my head up toward Max. He breathes deeply, watching me through hooded eyes.

"My apologies, I've never seen a man's bare chest before the two of you. Not up close, anyway."

"Do you enjoy it?" he asks, voice strained.

"Quite a lot, actually. Is yours identical, Leo?" I shift to address him.

Wordlessly, he responds by leaning back and undoing the top of his tunic, exposing a striking-ly similar, though slightly less bulky chest—more lean than his brother, but defined just the same.

"Max has always been more physically active. We possess tomes detailing ancient techniques useful for defending against attackers, and he has studied them well," Leo explains as I roll to lay my palm against his warm skin.

Max trails his hand down my side as I explore the planes of his brother's exposed torso. The taper of his waist is slightly sharper, almost un-noticeable until you're this close. Faintly, his hips jerk, showcasing his arousal. I swallow hard, con-sciously aware of the position I'm in.

Frazzled and uncertain, I remove my hand from Leo's skin and right myself, moving to the end of the bed. They each sit up and lean against the headboard, eyes drinking me in like crisp, cold water at the end of a long walk through arid fields.

"I..." The urge to tip my head down and shy away is strong, but I persist, meeting their gazes. "I don't wish to be intimate at the moment." Pride consumes me as I state my limitations, albeit less direct than I would like.

"If that is your wish," Leo says.

"Would you prefer that we cover ourselves?" Max asks, voice timid.

"I enjoy your bodies. I would still like to look at and admire you. But I understand it is unfair."

"You could never be unfair to us, so long as we get to enjoy your presence," Leo explains, a soft smile on his face.

"We shall wait as long as you need, Dearest." Max nods with an adoring smirk.

"And what if I'm never prepared? I-I would like to be intimate with each of you again..." I chew my lip. "But I cannot convince my mind that it is acceptable. Do you understand that all of this—" I gesture to the two of them, the room surrounding us. "—goes against all that I was raised to believe? I was not brought up in the manner that you were."

They move instantly as I begin to breathe irregularly. Leo holds me against his chest, and Max rubs my lower back with firm, steady pressure.

"We are fully aware. It will take more than a couple of days to adjust. You're allowed to question everything. I encourage you to," Leo murmurs in my ear, lying back with me against him.

"If the damage is irreparable, we would still gladly give our lives to love you as much as you're willing to allow." Max kisses my shoulder.

"Do each of you truly feel love for me?" I go still between them.

Silence suffocates the room as I await their responses. I'm keenly aware of the faintest bit of motion as they share undecipherable looks above me. I inhale a hefty breath, blowing it out through trembling lips.

"Would you like the simple answer?" Leo asks.

"Or would you prefer our deep, heartfelt confessions?" Max adds behind me, voice just above a whisper against my hair.

"Would you feel the same if I were another woman? Is your love for me merely a matter of convenience?"

"Phoebe, might I remind you that it took Leo months of heated arguments with the Guides to procure the rights to marry *you*..." Max explains gently.

"And," Leo begins, "in the process of doing so, Max was nearly banished. Meaning I was nearly banished."

"What?!" I gasp, turning in Leo's arms to face his brother. "How on Earth did that occur?"

"I saw you. I haven't gone to the community in years—not since our parents were sent into the wastes—but Leo had told me what the Guides said when he first made the proposal to them. I ventured to the community, and there you were. Auburn hair tied to the side in a messy braid, eyes nearly swollen shut and bruised. You appeared so frail, but your energy was vibrant. Of all the women I've ever seen, no other has brightened my life as you did in that moment."

His words make me feel weightless, as though I will float away if they let me go.

"He *may* have punched a guard in the face as he was being restrained for attempting to fight every single Guide for rejecting the proposal." Leo chuckles.

"Max?! Knowing the two of you, I would assume that you would have attempted to assault the Guides, Leo." My jaw will not close; I'm utterly taken aback.

"Oh, I would have done *so* much worse had they spoken to *me* about you as they did Max." A gravelly rumble accompanies Leo's words, threatening and sharp.

Arousing.

"But we're a peaceful community. The only weapons I've ever seen are hanging on the walls of your study. I don't know what more you could have done to them."

"Oh, historians do house the only weapons, and I'm *very* familiar with how to handle them." The intensity of his tone makes my core ache.

I'm officially convinced that this man will legitimately kill for me if the situation requires it. Max, more emotional and tender, *has* actually fought a man for me.

Realization sits heavily in my stomach. Aside from the stories Leo has read to me, I do not understand how love feels, what it does to people. Their parents walked out of the community, into certain death in the name of love.

Do I want to feel something that could be so detrimental to my health, cost me my life?

Why would anyone?

Still, my body yearns for theirs in ways I cannot understand. But what of my mind?

If my being desires them so, why can't I allow it to happen? Their lies and betrayal feel like ages ago, even though it's only been days. Each of them has been attentive, respectful, and never once pressed me for *more*.

Powers Above, I must be eternally fractured.

Some wife I've turned out to be. Trained for a lifetime to be the perfect image of loyalty and worthiness, putting all of my spare energy into skill studies and showcasing how well-behaved I am.

For what?

My saviors expect me to become a martyr.

I shrug out of their hold and stand from the bed as the war rages inside my mind.

If they speak to me as I leave, I'm unable to hear them. My pulse slams against my skull, deafening and chaotic. The hallway feels infinite as I drag my feet along the floor. The edges of my vision turn blurry as my breathing becomes erratic.

Stopping to grip the kitchen counter, I have a moment of clarity.

When did I get here?

Leo and Max call after me, but grant me space as I toss a hand back at them. When I round the corner into the hallway where *my* room is, I trudge forward. The door is still off the hinges from days ago, the visual reminder of their lies compounds my panic.

I think I'm crying, my face is too numb to be sure.

I finally make it to my bed, stiff and cold compared to the one I share with *them.* Curling into the smallest possible ball, I encase myself with the large blanket and wail. The weight of this life—the reality of this world—crashes down upon me.

Quietly, I chant, "Why me? Why me? Why me?" Through trembling lips. Cold, freezing cold, loneliness engulfs me despite the covers.

What is wrong with you, Phoebe?

Of all the lives I could have been given, why must this be the one?

"I've tried," I grit out, abundantly aware that they've followed me. "I've tried to come to terms with this... this situation." My voice cracks as I choke on tears. "I-I want you, but the thought is utterly terrifying. Why must you want me so badly?"

The mattress dips on either side of me as they sit.

Silence stretches for what feels like hours between us. They say nothing as I continue to crumble.

"Surely you do not want a woman like me. I am but a tattered shell. The Guides are wise and all-knowing, there is a good reason they attempted to keep you from making this mistake." I heave, emotions churning like vile rations in my stomach.

"Phoebe," Leo warns, voice low, "you are remarkable. I've meant it every time I've said it. No other woman in New Promise compares to *you*. I love you and do *not* enjoy hearing you speak so poorly of yourself."

"You're highly intelligent, compassionate, and determined. We've been in love with the mere thought of you since we had the chance. Having the real thing only escalated our feelings." Max places a hand on my shoulder through the blanket.

"I-I do not know how to feel love. I also do not know if I would be prepared to die for either of you at this moment," I sputter, swallowing down my cries.

"That is perfectly acceptable. All of this is new and foreign to you. As we've stated previously, there is no deadline or expectation. If you never love us, we will accept it. That will not change how we feel about you." Leo finds my other shoulder and squeezes. "I love you, Phoebe Koeler, in spite of New Promise, in spite of the Guides and their laws. Nothing, no one, and no amount of time will change that."

"If you were to ask it of me, I'd go fight the entirety of the Guides *and* their puny guard force. If it would make you happy, I would walk to the ends of the Earth—through wasteland and hardship—to procure the last squash alive, because I love you." Max chuckles. "Despite the looming danger, I'd face it all for you."

The room falls into silence once more. My breathing calms as I digest their words. Slowly, I pull the blankets off my face. Puffy eyes, runny nose, and all, they look at me as if I'm the most precious of artifacts. Soft and warm, their faces bring me the familiar comfort I've come to appreciate.

"I must be utterly repulsive. Please do not look at me in such a way." I scowl, wiping my eyes.

"I'm proud of your progress, Darling." Leo produces a handkerchief and hands it to me.

"As am I, that was your most severe panic yet, and you did not faint." Max gently runs his fingers through my hair.

I pause, looking to each of them. "I... I didn't!" I sit up straight and smile brightly at them, woes washing away as I celebrate the small victory. "All my life, I've suffered and been punished for my fainting spells. They called me a fake, a liar, told me I was destined to fail because I could not handle womanhood." I twirl the handkerchief in my hands and stare at the wall.

"You're the picture of womanhood; powerful, loyal, courageous." Leo scoots closer, pulling me into his arms. "They know nothing of your strength and resilience."

Max slides up to my other side, wrapping himself around me. "They're all cowards, lost in olden ways. Too afraid to deviate from twisted traditions. Women are humans, just as men. Why society has labeled you as house tenders and child bearers alone is a mystery. You are so much more."

Flutters come to life inside me. I turn to Leo, and his eyes scan my face, asking a silent question. I answer by pressing my lips against his, just for a moment. As I pull away, he attempts to follow, but I turn my head to Max and kiss him as well. He inhales sharply through his nose, releasing a dreamy sigh as I pull away.

"I want to love you. I *will* love you both someday. Even if it costs me my life."

They each kiss my cheek and I giggle softly at the sensation.

Being between them causes my body to tingle.

I'm done fighting this, my mind will have to concede.

Soft kisses on my forehead and nose pull a smile across my lips. I stretch and peel my puffy eyes open. Leo is lying face to face with me, hand brushing my cheek. "Good morning, Darling." His eyes light up as he smiles.

I blink away the sleep and hum contentedly. When I roll to address Max, he's surprisingly absent. Turning back toward Leo, brows pinched together, I open my mouth to speak, but nothing comes out.

"Surely you're thirsty, one moment." Leo sits up and produces a glass of water from the nightstand. "Here, have a drink. Max is in the kitchen preparing breakfast."

I right myself and sip down some of the refreshingly cold liquid.

"Breakfast?" I force out, voice still ragged.

"Yes, we stayed in bed with you all day. You exhausted yourself. We wanted to ensure you rested and recovered. But nearly twenty-four hours have elapsed. It would be irresponsible not to wake you at this point."

"I-I slept for an entire day?" I rub my temples. "I do not feel rested."

"You've likely overslept. We attempted to wake you for dinner last night, but it was of no use." He takes the empty glass from me after I swallow the rest of the water.

"You both simply... stayed here with me?"

"For the first several hours, yes. Eventually, we had duties to take care of, but did so in waves. He would lie with you for a couple of hours, and I would take the next shift. After dinner, we made do with fitting the three of us in this small bed." He scrunches his face up.

"Why did you not carry me to our room? It wouldn't be the first, or even the second, occasion." I tip my head in question.

"We were unsure if that would be acceptable, given how upset you were. For fear of causing more emotional distress, we opted for a night of discomfort instead." His full lips pull into a tight frown.

"I appreciate the consideration, but I'm quite alright," I respond. Fortunately, my voice holds up and helps me get my point across.

"Good morning, Dearest," Max announces as he approaches the doorless threshold to my room. "I made some sauteed squash with fresh herbs and fried eggs for everyone. Would you like to eat in bed?" He meets my eyes for a moment and swiftly looks away.

"That sounds lovely. I would quite enjoy a breakfast in bed. Exactly like we hear about in the stories Leo reads." I beam at him and watch the flurry of emotions cross his face before he nods, offers me a timid smile in return, and steps away.

I shift on the bed, allowing Leo space to sit. He joins me and laces his fingers through mine as I rest my head on his shoulder.

Max returns in an instant, tray filled with plates of food in hand. He stands at the foot of my bed, looking between us. I offer him a tender smile and pat the empty side of my mattress. He places our food on the stand next to him and sits, expression filled with uncertainty.

He grabs a plate and hands it to Leo, then sighs before speaking. "Are you not angry with us? I apologize profusely if I've been overbearing with my affection. My intention is never to upset you."

"My sweet Maximus." I turn to him, and he pauses, my plate suspended mid-air. "I am who upset me. The two of you have shown me more kindness than I've ever known. If anyone is to apologize, it is I. You're wonderful. I truly appreciate all that you do for me."

"You cannot help the way you were raised, Darling, a lifetime of being taught that only a man's needs and happiness matter will not be unlearned in just a couple of months," Leo speaks up.

I direct my attention to him and continue. "You are correct, I can not. However, what I *can* control is who I am now. From this moment, I vow to love each of you. Someday, somehow, I will make it so."

Max inhales a sudden breath, blowing out harshly. Leo, ever intense, pulls me onto his lap. Positioning me over him, he stops just before our mouths meet.

"Does this mean we can kiss you whenever it suits us? Because I've been longing to feel your lips on mine again."

"It has only been two days," I whisper with a slight laugh.

"Days of torture, Darling. Please end my suffering."

Max slides his hand up my spine, and I shift my gaze to find him watching intently—my plate back on the tray, forgotten. The anticipation alight on his face as he spectates does me in. I close the final gap between my tingling lips and Leo's, moaning as his tongue explores my mouth.

Before I'm allowed to get carried away, he pulls back and lifts me effortlessly, directing me to Max and his waiting arms. No words are required. We fall into a softer, but no less satisfying, kiss. As my hands find his shoulders, he, too, pulls away.

Unnaturally frustrated, I whine as he returns me to my seat.

"Dearest, you must be famished. Please, eat before it gets cold."

"But—"

"We have a lifetime for kissing and loving one another. Please eat for us," Leo insists and I know there is no use arguing.

"It smells amazing. Thank you again." I take the plate from Max and groan at the first bite.

"It pleases me to hear your sounds of appreciation," Max says around his food, grinning as he chews.

Leo is the first to finish and leaves without warning. Electric bolts shoot through me, assuming I've upset him.

But how?

Have I given too much of my time to Max? Perhaps Leo would also enjoy some praise? Navigating this relationship is already proving to be a challenge. How do I ensure their happiness?

As I stare at my food and contemplate my best course of action, Leo returns. My eyes widen as they land on the book in his hand.

"I'd like to finish the story we have been enjoying, if that would be acceptable. We're nearly at their happy ending." He smiles and comes to sit back down.

I blink rapidly at him. "You're not angry or jealous?" I ask, head tipped toward him.

"What, may I ask, would lead you to believe I am? Have I expressed any negative feelings?" He pinches his brows together, head rearing back slightly.

"You silently excused yourself, and I've only ever known my father to do as such just before an outburst. I had concluded that something I said to Max must have grated on your nerves. I apologize for misjudging your actions." I pull the corner of my lip between my teeth.

Leo chuckles, filled with adoration. "Darling, I will never feel jealousy or envy of you and your relations with Max."

"And I will never feel negatively about your time with Leo. I quite enjoy seeing you with him," Max agrees.

"You do?" I swallow hard.

"It's a mutual enjoyment," Leo answers. "Watching the way your body reacts to him is as if I get a front-row seat to my own personal pornography."

"Pornography? Are you referring to the sexual art that men use to relieve their needs when their wives are unavailable?"

"That is how the community views it, yes. But with you, it's as if I'm watching myself love you the way I wish I could," Max explains, voice tentative and laced with shame.

"What does that mean, Max? You have made love to me." I twist my face tightly.

"But not in the way Leo did. I could never demand such things or take you so roughly." His face falls, eyes darting away from mine.

"The way you love me is perfect. Never compare yourself to another. You may look nearly identical, and have lived your lives pretending to be the same person, but you're not." I take his hand, holding his gaze hostage as it darts to mine. "You're allowed to have your own way of loving me. I enjoy it just the same." I turn to Leo and continue, "The same goes for you. Please never see the way Max loves me and assume you're inferior. I quite enjoy your differences. You're *not* the same person, and I would not expect you to love me like you are."

Leo grips my jaw, eyes hardened—looking *directly* at me. "I must insist that you finish your breakfast, I'll read to you as you enjoy it. And then, when you're done, we shall move this conversation to *our* room—*our* bed."

I swallow a moan, panting in his grasp.

"Would that be acceptable to you, my Darling?" He tips his chin, looking down at me.

"Yes," I breathe out.

"Are you sure that you're prepared for us? Do you have any clue what you're asking for?" His voice is low, thick like the haze in my mind.

"Yes," I whimper.

"Very well. Enjoy your meal." As his hand leaves my face, I whirl to meet Max's languid gaze.

I reach over him, taking my plate from the stand. Leo reads slowly while I try to eat. Max grips my thigh, trailing his fingertips along the crease. My skin burns under his simple touch.

He won't meet my eye, but doesn't stop as we continue to listen. I drop my fork as his hand glides higher. My breathing stops, anticipating more... but it doesn't come. Instead, Leo pauses his reading, and Max waits for me to lift my fork again. As I skewer a chunk of delectable squash, they each resume.

So this is the game they wish to play.

It seems the only way I'll get any relief is if I obey. Ironic, considering my obedience was meticulously programmed over nearly two decades of precise training regimens.

Now I only wish to defy them and see what may come of it.

I intentionally set my fork down and grab hold of Max's swollen manhood. His hips jerk from the contact, and he thrusts into my hand against his own will. Shuddering, he grips my thigh as I work him in my palm, tossing his head back with a gravelly moan.

Leo sets his book on the side table and pulls me away from his brother, careful not to spill my food. "How unfair of you to tease him." His grip on my waist grows tighter. "Just for that, I will make you beg for release... after you finish eating."

"But—"

"You will need the energy. Please trust me." He grabs hold of my fork and feeds me a large portion of egg. "Once this plate is clear, I'll carry you to the bed, then you're ours." A promising growl laces his declaration.

Oddly enough, where I may have been intimidated by it yesterday, I'm aching at the thought now. Some final part of my subconscious finally seems to have caught up.

They're *mine*. And I'm ready for them.

Leo carries me through the doorway of our bedroom, lays me down and I sink comfortably into the plush mattress. As I look up at him, he stands tall and directs his attention to Max.

"Take her tunic off, slowly." He licks his lips and watches with undivided attention as his brother crawls up to me, carefully undoing my upper tie. As my breasts are exposed to him, his eyes flash with desire, hand trailing between them on its way down to my waist sash.

"They're perfect, like the rest of her, aren't they?" Leo asks, now sitting in a chair at the foot of the bed.

"So very perfect," Max praises, undoing the knot at my hip. "I'm honored to be this close to you again, Dearest." He kisses near my navel as I'm fully exposed to them.

"Very good, now it is your turn." Leo has already undone the front of his tunic, manhood on full display as he lazily works himself.

Max follows his instructions without hesitation. Under his brother's guidance, he's much more self-assured, far less intimidated by my presence. As his hardness is bared to me, I understand the difference I felt before. He *is* thicker than Leo, though slightly shorter. The stretch of him was more noticeable for a reason. Still, they're both very impressive, all natural as The Powers Above demand.

I look between them, trying to swallow as my mouth goes dry.

"Darling, this is all for you. I can practically hear the intimidation running through your mind. *We* are here to please *you*." Leo stands and strolls to join us on the bed. "I'm going to have Max take you until you're a mess, and only then will I join." He brushes his nose against my cheek and looks to his brother. "Kiss her, and get your hands dirty, just how you've dreamed of."

With never-before-expressed confidence, Max shifts over me, pressing his mouth to mine like I'm holding his last breath hostage. Hungry for any sort of relief, I drag my nails slowly up and down his back, pressing my hips upward. He shivers atop me, nipping at my lower lip as I seek much-needed friction.

Slowly, his right hand trails back to my breasts, cupping one and pinching at my oversensitive nipple. My back arches and I moan into his mouth, pulling a groan from Leo. As I look his way, I see him gripping himself, stroking the entire length of his erection as he watches.

"Keep teasing her, Max. Let her ache for us." His words come out strained through faint grunts.

Just as he's told, my torturer trails his fingers back up to my collarbone, following the slope before slipping down to my nipple again and twirling around it. Our kiss breaks as I whimper, scowling as much as I can manage. I lift my hips once more, eager for any sensation, but find none.

"Please?" I offer him a pitiful look, hoping he'll show some mercy.

"Listen to her. She's being so good for us, and I'm feeling gracious." A simple command from Leo, and Max brings his hand lower, teasing as he lightly drags a finger along the crease of my thigh.

"Do you want this?" he asks, voice more ragged than I've ever heard. Before I can answer, he slides a single finger inside me. As he returns his lips to mine and works against my sensitive inner spots, Leo has other ideas.

"Taste her. She'll be your favorite flavor, I can assure you of that." He breathes out, stroking faster as his brother nods and descends.

Hot kisses trail slowly down my chest, stomach, and core. Once Max is settled between my thighs, still working his fingers inside of me, he swipes the tip of his tongue slowly through my wetness. My grip immediately finds his hair, pulling gently at first. The sensation increases his efforts, and before long, I'm tugging harder as he sucks on my swollen clit.

Leo pants beside us, working himself faster. "Bring her all the way, Max, let us hear her."

Thrusting his fingers into me more intently, he continues lavishing my clit until I feel the coil in my core snap. I cry out his name, holding tight to his hair as he coaxes me through a life-altering climax.

Gasping for air, he tears his face away from my nether regions, bare chest heaving. Leaning back on his knees, he strokes himself twice and releases on my stomach, immediately red with embarrassment. My first instinct is to comfort him, to reassure him that he's done a phenomenal job.

As I move to sit, Leo grabs my jaw, turning me toward him and stops me.

"He'll be ready again in a moment, don't worry," he whispers with an impish smirk. "Roll over, Darling. It's my turn to make you squirm."

I look at Max, laid out across the foot of the bed, and he offers me a sated smile accompanied by a slight nod. With his silent permission, I shift to my knees with a raised brow.

Leo places my face in the pillows and runs his hands over the roundness of my backside. "You'll not concern yourself with our pleasure today, Darling. Everything we do is for you, remember?" He inserts two fingers into my throbbing center and begins thrusting.

Crazed by the sensations, I attempt to move away, but he grips my hip with his free hand, holding me in place. As I beg him to stop, give me but a moment of reprieve, he increases his pace. I nearly break free from his hold, and he lets up, groaning while I throb around his fingers.

"Max, would you kindly hold our wife?" he asks as if I'm not crying frenzied tears from the sensations he's caused.

"Do you want this to stop?" Max asks as he slides up beside me, rolling onto his back to pull me atop him.

"She has not said to stop, despite her best efforts to escape," Leo pants, running his hands over my thighs as he leans in to kiss my lower back.

"You've rendered her speechless," Max says as he runs his fingers along my sweat-drenched scalp. "This is a beautiful look for you, Dearest."

"Mmmm." The only sound I can manage as I stare lazily into his gentle gaze. I tip my head up toward him and press our lips together.

"See, she is perfectly fine. Allow me to retrieve some water for us, and we can continue." Leo, fully nude and very erect, walks out of the room, leaving Max to my care.

Max, who is already aroused and ready for me again.

Starved for him, I trail my hand down his front to take hold of his thick erection, and he gasps against my lips. I work him for a few moments, savoring all of his small grunts of pleasure. He thrusts into my hand as I tighten my grip, biting his lip as he struggles to maintain control.

"What a glorious sight," Leo says on a groan as he returns. He hands us each a glass of cool water, and we drink quickly.

The brief intermission does nothing to ease the amount of sexual tension filling the air. I'm still straddling Max, his erection nestled between us as Leo sits next to us on the mattress. I turn toward him, and he wastes no time claiming my lips in a deep, hungry kiss.

As he watches, Max grips my hips and drags my core along his swollen manhood. I whimper, but Leo swallows it down until my hand finds his erection and takes hold. His head falls back as I trail my finger under his foreskin. Max thrusts against me, nearly slipping inside from the angle, and I gasp.

"Please," I breathe out, eager to *feel* one of them. I'd even consider trying both if it meant this perpetual state of teasing would end.

"Who do you want to fall apart on first?" Leo forces out, voice thick with need.

Instead of offering a reply, I lift myself, taking all of Max in a swift motion. He moans, biting his lip as his head falls back. Leo breaks our contact and shifts to move behind me. Slinking his hand between my body and his brother's, he works my clit and helps me please myself while Max lays back, thrusting into me in rhythm with my motions.

"Leo," I plead, filled with raw desire. "B-both. I... need." Rolling my hips against Max, I tremble as Leo's touch leaves.

"Both? Would you like me inside you as well? Or is your rear entrance in need of stimulation?" He grips my hips, eagerly awaiting my reply.

"W-with Max." I look to his brother below me, who groans as the words leave my mouth.

I'm unsure where this reckless, feverish need has come from, but I've chosen not to argue with my body's wishes.

I feel one of Leo's fingers at my entrance, gently easing in. "I must prepare you for this; you're not practiced, regardless of how many orgasms you've had." He continues to stretch me, adding another finger and working until he can fit a third.

By the time I'm a writing mess, Max is on the brink of insanity. "Guide's mercy, Dearest, I do *not* think I'll last long," he whimpers as the head of Leo's manhood nudges my entrance. He stills below me, allowing his brother to enter me slowly.

"I will enjoy myself regardless, I just need to feel you both." I wince as Leo pushes in the slightest amount.

"Are you positive you *can?*" Max asks, breathing irregularly as the space inside me grows even fuller.

"I'm nearly there, Darling. You're doing such a spectacular job," Leo's warm hand finds the small of my back as he presses the last couple of inches inside with a satisfied growl.

Max grunts below me as I try to catch my breath, filled beyond my wildest dreams. Gently, feeling out the situation, I move, and they both shudder.

Leo is the first to thrust, slipping out of me ever so slightly and pushing back in. Max, eyes closed as he centers himself, thrusts opposite him. Something in the way my incoherent moans break the silence in the room gives them all the confirmation they need. Together, they find an immaculate rhythm.

Max grows frenzied, taking one of my nipples in his mouth as he increases the force of his movements. Leo drives himself as deeply as possible, allowing his brother the moment. I press myself into the two of them as he continues. The pressure, the sensations, are almost too much as he hits just the right spot inside of me, bringing me to a screaming climax.

Letting out a strangled sound, he follows shortly after, spilling deep inside of me. As we both struggle to catch our breath, Leo continues slowly moving, moaning my name as he fills me with his own release.

We lay still as the moments pass us by, nothing more than the sounds of our erratic breaths filling the room. Finally, Leo finds the will to move, leaning back and kissing my shoulder gently before slowly sliding out of me. At the sensation, I wince and settle back into Max's steadily rising chest.

"I'll return in just a moment. Stay there." Leo excuses himself and walks out into the hall.

I lay my head down to listen to the rapid beating of Max's heart against my cheek. He wraps his arms around me and releases a contented sigh—one I return with equal adoration. Some part of me feels repaired by what we've just done, despite the tenderness between my thighs.

Our attention shifts to Leo as he returns with damp rags and more chilled water. "Darling, are you feeling alright? That was far more than I had expected you would want." He helps me off Max.

I wince as the two of them clean me up, wiping away the proof of our deviance.

What would my teachers say?

No, I cannot continue falling back into the mind-set they forced upon me. Especially not now that I've given myself to this new reality and am smitten by the men tending to my thoroughly pleased lady bits.

"Dearest?" Max stops and places a hand on my cheek. "Are you?"

"Oh, I am fantastic." I laugh, still breathless. "I may need a few days before we attempt anything of the sort again. But I can *not* wait to do that some more." Making my best attempt at a smile, I close my eyes as they finish cleaning up.

Leo chuckles softly and hands me a glass. "Do drink some water, you exerted a lot of energy, we all did. Max, are you going to feel up to making food later? We've been at it for a couple of hours in here." He sits beside me on the bed, pulling me into his side.

"Not to worry, I'll ensure we're all fed," he answers with a soft, loving smile as he curls into my other side.

I'd do just about anything to live in this moment forever. There's officially no going back for me.

'16

Yesterday was the beginning of something new and different. Both of my men have been increasingly affectionate, kissing me on the cheek in passing, stopping for quick embraces as we work on tasks together. When we cooked breakfast this morning, Leo even wrapped his arms around me and rested his chin on my shoulder.

They've invited me to the catacombs, and I'm curious why. Normally, I'm welcome to join them as I wish, but they never formally request my presence. My heart flutters thinking about what they must have planned for me.

After how gentle and attentive they've been, I no longer believe they will harm me, so their intentions are exciting in ways I cannot put into words.

I enter the study and find them sitting in the two old chairs. They stand to greet me, each kissing a cheek as I approach. Strange energy, tense and uncertain, fills the normally quaint room. The excitement that had taken up residence in my stomach dwindles slightly. Perhaps I have misjudged this invitation. There is a small chance that they're about to devastate me, or completely blindside me with horrible news. There is only one way to know for sure.

"Shall we?" I ask, motioning to the hidden hatch.

Silently, they nod in unison, ushering me toward the far corner where the entrance lies.

Leo opens it, and Max leads the way, helping me down the first few steps. As the three of us descend the long staircase to the bottom, my questions multiply. They're never this quiet. Something peculiar is afoot.

The decoy room has been decorated with a plethora of strange items. Laid out across an ancient table, sitting in the middle of the room, is a collection of various tomes. A large map spans the back wall, just next to where the door opens up into the chasm. My brows knit together as I inspect the materials; the tomes are handwritten and appear to be far newer than expected. I lift one and read a highlighted sentence, dropping it instantly.

As Leo and Max come to my side, I tremble. I know the meaning of the words, but they make no sense to me.

"Phoebe, we're doing this because we love you." Leo places a hand on my shoulder.

"I-I do not understand," I choke out.

"It is a lot to take in, and this is only the beginning," Max explains, voice soft, as he embraces me from behind.

With his warmth to comfort me, my mind relaxes slightly. "Who wrote this? What do they mean by 'It's all a lie'? This does not look ancient."

"That is because it's not." Leo moves to sit at the table, grabbing another of the tomes. "These journals are contraband. We found them buried deep in the catacombs, surely placed there with the intent of nobody ever stumbling across them."

"What?!" I shriek, startling in Max's arms.

"They belong to persons unknown, erased from our history, though the dates are merely from about one hundred years ago. Those who wrote them had been beyond these walls and lived to tell the tale," Leo continues.

"You—how long have you known about this?"

"Honestly, for quite some time," Max answers, squeezing me slightly. "We meant to tell you..." His voice gets soft.

"But?!" I ask harshly, and Leo is quick to speak up.

"Your well-being was far more important. This—" He motions to the setup around us. "—is not going anywhere. You, on the other hand, were in need of our time, our energy, our presence. Nothing in this world is of more importance to us than you." He stands and comes to face me. "Our duties can wait, your happiness will not." He cups my jaw in his hand.

Max releases his hold on me, and I fall into Leo as he pulls me into a dizzying kiss. My body presses against him, conforming perfectly. As we pull apart, I forget for a moment why we were here, until I spot Max sitting at the table, skimming through another tome.

Right, apparently everything is a lie.

"So..." I chew my lip, walking slowly toward him. "What exactly is all of this?" My heart hammers wildly, but I manage to quell the building panic.

Leo steps to my side and exchanges a look with Max, more of their silent conversation passes before my eyes. It's quite intriguing to witness, albeit slightly annoying to feel left out. I fold my arms over and tap my foot, causing Max to chuckle.

Leo places a hand on my shoulder and inhales. "Phoebe, do you remember when you first came here?"

"It has not even been two full months, of course I do. I'm not senile," I deadpan.

Max snorts in his seat.

"Pardon my lack of specifics. I mean, do you remember when I told you that I don't quite believe the world is as lost as the Guides lead the citizens of New Promise to believe?"

"Oh. I do faintly recall, yes." It was such a one-off, passive comment, and I've had much more pressing matters to concern myself with. But I do.

"Well, the catacombs we tend are vast, as you've seen. Max and I have been digging around. In our various shifts, we uncovered these tomes." He lifts a tome, turning to a tabbed entry. "Someone before us placed these journals here. I'm not sure the Guides are aware of their existence. They seem to be written records of some previous explorers. This one, Reginald Chance, outlines a beautiful and thriving life outside of these stone walls."

"Why would they come back?" The question falls out of my mouth in an instant, the meaning clear. We all know I'd never consider returning here if I were to leave and survive to witness a vibrant, joyous life.

Max speaks up, "Based on entries, they attempted to return and reveal the truth—" He swallows hard. "—and the Guides had them executed for it."

"You would think so cruelly of the Guides?" I ask.

"Would you not? Having finally seen what the monthly meetings entail, you would believe them to be kind and forgiving?" Leo interjects, "These writings explain the wonders of the outside world in great detail. Some even have hand-drawn illustrations of new settlements that have been built. They describe scenes of wilderness thriving, people living pleasant lives free of overbearing leadership."

"Are you suggesting that the Guides are liars? Is this why that tome was turned to the page stating such?"

"Yes," they answer together.

Closing my eyes, I brace myself on the table. After a few steadying breaths, I square my shoulders and address them, "What is it you plan to do with this information? How are we to escape?"

They exchange yet another look, but this one is easily readable, shock. Mouths slightly agape, eyes widened.

"May I ask what has you so surprised?" I place a hand on my hip. "You expected me to crumble and panic?"

"It's not that we didn't think you'd believe us," Max starts, "we just anticipated having to explain our goals."

"The plan, Darling, should you decide to accompany us, is simple." Leo opens another tome, showing the gate. New Promise's one and only way in or—in most cases—out. Few have actually *seen* the gate. Many believe it's purely a fable made up to frighten the youth into behaving.

Fathers will tell their children that they'll send them out the gate if they disobey. In training, our teachers would inform us that the gate was the worst form of punishment, that we would be for-

tunate if our future husband pushes our button should we require discipline. I stare at the
words, and my stomach falls to the floor.

"If the gate is real, and the world outside of
New Promise is habitable, we just need to get
exiled, correct?" I turn to them, straightening
where I stand.

"You're irresistible when you think the same
way we do, Darling." Leo kisses me hard, hands
pulling my waist against him as I lose myself. I
sway on my feet as he releases me, and a blissful
smile spreads across my face.

Max beams at us from his seat and motions for
me to join him. I stroll over and sit on his lap.

He softly presses his lips against my cheek
and twirls the end of my hair around his finger.
"Dearest, would you like to train with us? We
expect some resistance along the way. I'd love
to show you some of the combat techniques I've
learned. Leo is a weapons master, and I'm sure
he could teach you how to wield a dagger like a
professional."

"If it's an excuse to spend more time with the
two of you, I'll gladly accept." I cast a smile at
both of them.

"I'm astonished at how easily you've agreed
to run away with us. What if these tomes are
wrong and we perish?" Leo asks.

"Then I'd perish knowing I tried to free myself of this oppressive community built on lies."

"Guide's mercy, you can't keep speaking in such a seductive manner." He groans, scrubbing a hand over his face, and I chuckle.

Max opens the tome nearest him and shows me a passage, my eyes crinkle from the smile that takes over my face. "Are those drawings of different animals?"

"Indeed. There seem to be quite a few species that have survived. Far more than the cattle, swine, and hens we know."

I take a moment to contemplate and consider the repercussions of this scheme... One wrong step in the wastes could prove fatal, but the chance at a better life for all of us is worth it. My love for hens and excitement for all the other animals we may encounter are mere bonuses.

Decision made, I straighten my spine. "Well then, that settles it. Let's get to work, husbands!" I clap my hands together and they let out laughs from deep within their chests.

We gather around the table, scouring tomes for more information on the gate and banishment. The *how* seems easy enough. There are two of them, and that's an offense of banishing-worthy proportions in and of itself. Once the Guides learn that they removed my execution capsule—which hasn't been done yet, but they plan to—they'll throw me out alongside them.

It's not until my stomach rumbles loudly that we realize how much time has passed. We neatly collect all our notes and pack everything away into the safety of the catacombs before ascending back to our dwelling.

Max and I prepare dinner—a lovely medley of pan-seared vegetables and breast of hen—and the three of us gather around the table. As the weight of today's revelation settles in, I sigh, leaning back in my chair.

"Darling, are you not feeling well? Should we run you a bath?" Leo asks, forkful of food suspended in mid-air as he awaits my reply.

"No, I'm just overcome with the reality that my life as I know it, yet again, will be completely redefined." I lean my head back and stare at the ceiling.

"While that may be true, this time it will be for the best," he offers in a warm tone.

"He's telling the truth, Dearest. Imagine a world where we can love each other freely, in the light of day. We won't need to hide away in this hole in the ground. No Guides to keep us in line with the terms set by The Powers Above. No fear of death if we step out of line. Imagine the animals and all the other vegetables we can grow!" Max rambles on, excitement coating every word.

I look at him and feel a bright grin overtake my face. "I adore the way you show your emotions. You're such a lighthearted and fun-loving man. Never change, Maximus." At my praise, he pulls his lower lip into his mouth, cheeks turning a vibrant shade of red. "I especially love how much you blush over the faintest praise and flirtation. It was the first thing that made me think Leo had a whole separate personality, before I knew he was an entirely different *person*." I chuckle.

"He has always been the bashful one and the jokester," Leo replies with a hint of humor in his tone.

"And you're the furthest thing from bashful, mister forward," I poke back. "I love how upfront and honest you are. Even if it can be upsetting, I never have to wonder about my standing when you're around." I inhale deeply through my nose and sit up straight. "What I'm leading up to is that, given everything that happened today, I have come to realize that I *love* you. Both of you. When you told me the plan to escape, the first thing that crossed my mind was, 'When do we leave?' because I'm going wherever you go. There's nothing for me here, and you're everything I care about, anyway."

In the blink of an eye, they're at my sides, lips pressed against my cheeks. The silly, uncanny things they do like this always make me laugh.

Despite their differences, they still share the same inclinations; it's rather entertaining.

As they pull away, I give each of them a *real* kiss. We clear our plates and clean up, Leo carries me to the bath, and they *thoroughly* pamper me.

Tonight we celebrate love, because tomorrow we begin planning to escape the lies we've been fed.

Buzzing energy fills the catacombs today. I can imagine that Max and Leo have already thought out all of the details, but I haven't the faintest idea of how we're to proceed. Fortunately, we have ample time to prepare, as nobody is aware that we know the truth about the outside world.

A kinder person than I might consider trying to rally fellow citizens, but I know they'd never trust us over the Guides. They're the peacekeepers, our modern-day law enforcement, and the ones who keep the citizens fed. If I hadn't been thrust into this life of different views, I wouldn't trust my own words.

Even now, I'm only about ninety percent positive that we're making the correct decision. My men are convinced that these tomes are speaking the truth, and at this point, that is enough for me. The Guides have only ever viewed me the same as the rest of the community—the lowly daughter of Raymond Harding. In what instance would I chance my happiness and well-being for *any* of them? My one true friend was executed before my eyes. May this place burn.

Some may call me spiteful, so be it.

Max and I file into a side room, leaving Leo to his studies. He leads me to a small padded area of the floor, removes his shirt, and stretches his strong shoulders. Reaching each arm above his head, he rolls his neck from side to side. I'm fairly certain my breathing stops as I admire his form.

"You may want to consider limbering up as well. We'll be getting *very* physical... but not in the way your eyes tell me you're imagining." He smirks despite the redness of his cheeks and chest.

"Oh, right. I'm not sure exactly how I should be stretching. Would it be best to mimic you?"

Instead of answering, he strolls my way, circling me until he's pressed against my back. I gasp as his hands travel up my sides, fingers grazing my breasts. His confidence since we all became intimate has increased, despite his natural affinity for blushing. It's dizzying in an unfathomably attractive way.

Leaning in, he whispers, "Let's just do it together." Taking my hands in his, he brings our arms up high until I can no longer reach.

"Max, you're nearly a foot taller than me, please." I groan as my shoulders pull.

"I know, but a good stretch should hurt, just a slight amount."

Now it's my turn to blush, cheeks heating as my core clenches. I mold like the finest putty in his arms, allowing him to stretch my shoulders, hips, and back until he's satisfied with our warm-up.

"Welcome to your first lesson. We're primarily going to focus on a subcategory referred to as grappling. Instead of physically fighting, the idea is to subdue your assailant by immobilizing them. I shall demonstrate, then have you perform the grapple on me."

He turns to face me and places his palms on my shoulders. "Do the same," he instructs.

As I make contact, he takes hold of my left arm, twisting my wrist around, gently but effectively. "Once you have someone in this position, you're going to keep their hand held in yours and place your free hand on their elbow, forcing it to bend." Effortlessly, he wrenches my arm behind me and presses the back of my hand just below my shoulder blade. I hiss at the pull, thankful for the stretches. "Now, the higher you lift their hand, the more strain it will put on their shoulder, causing increased pain should they require correction."

He lets my arm go and waits for me to shake it out, regaining the lost circulation. "Your turn, show me what you've got, Dearest." He lunges, not giving me a second to think. With the instructions fresh in my mind, I take hold of his wrist and twist as he showed me, quickly bending his elbow and pinning his arm behind him. He grunts as I hold tight. "Beautiful, but please don't take all that rage out on me, save it for someone deserving, yeah?"

I blink and let him go. "Sorry, I don't intend to harm you." I reach up and massage the joint, staring into his eyes.

"I'll survive," he murmurs, eyes darting to my lips for a moment before clearing his throat. "That was adequate, but we should try a few more times to ensure you're comfortable with the maneuver."

After a half-dozen more, he rolls his shoulder and kisses my cheek. "You're a natural. We'll revisit tomorrow. Next, we'll cover leg sweeps. The most efficient way to immobilize an adversary is to knock them down. Even the largest of foes can be caught off guard and brought to the ground with a properly executed leg sweep. Once they're prone, you can apply the hammerlock we just learned, and they'll be nearly incapable of harming you, so long as their free arm is secured."

He shows me the proper stance to assume, dropping down, one knee bent, the other leg extended, and guides me through the proper motion to take someone down without knocking myself off balance. We cover a few more arm locks and wrist locks, as well as ground holds, before he stands and comes for me; no mercy and no warning.

My body acts on impulse, I raise my knee to his stomach and he doubles over, coughing as I drop down to take his legs out from under him. He grunts as the air leaves his lungs. Quickly, I move to roll him into a wrist lock and pull his arm behind him, straddling his back. Panting, I blink and register the position we're in.

I've done it!

A rush of laughter bursts out of me, and he joins in, out of breath, as I let go of his arm. He rolls beneath me, and I lean down to kiss him as my adrenaline fades.

"You continue to amaze me, Phoebe Koeler." His wonder-filled eyes shine in the dimly lit catacombs.

"I would be nothing without my wonderful instructor." I smile down at him, running my hands across his chest. "Sooooo," I start as he closes his eyes, sighing under my touch. "What else do you have planned for me today?"

"You're all mine for the rest of the afternoon, Darling," Leo says, leaning against the doorway as he watches us.

Startled, I tear my hands from Max. "H-how long have you been there?"

"Just long enough to wish I were the combat master." He chuckles. "I should have let it continue and enjoyed the show, but we must be vigilant with our training. It's only day one, after all."

"I apologize for uh..." I fidget with my tunic.

"For what? Enjoying a moment with one of your husbands? There is no need to feel guilty. Neither of us will be offended or upset by you being intimate with the other. You do not need to include both of us at all times. We enjoy it, but it's not a requirement."

I look at Max, and he nods with a soft expression. "You may be intimate with either of us as it suits you, Dearest. No rules or expectations."

"Well, in that case, I will stop worrying about upsetting either of you. This situation is still very new to me. I understand you've had your entire lives to figure out your limitations, or lack thereof, I have just stumbled into this." I stand up and dust myself off.

"And you're handling it with the grace I had expected." Leo pushes off the door frame and comes to me. "I'll never stop reminding you how remarkable you are." He pulls me into a deep kiss, stealing my just-recovered breath. As he pulls away, I meet his eyes and find pure adoration swirling within them. "Shall we continue to your weapons training? Ideally, you'll never need to trouble yourself with using one. However, should you require it, daggers are an exceptional choice. I've found a rather intricate ancient one that I think you'll love." He places a bound sheath in my palm.

I stare down at it in awe as he undoes the fastener, and a small, polished handle awaits. Black with ornate etchings, embellished with golden accents.

"It's beautiful," I breathe out, afraid to touch it for fear that I would somehow ruin its majesty.

"Take it out of the casing, the blade is equally magnificent," Leo encourages me. "Fear not, it won't harm you as long as you only grip the handle. See how it feels in your hand, and then I'll show you how to use it."

Slowly, as if it will startle and run off, I grasp the handle—smooth and perfectly fitted—and pull the blade free. Double-edged, curved, and shimmering, a blood-red stone is affixed to the very base near the handle. I hold my breath as I admire the detailed engravings down the center, some ancient runes I cannot decipher. "Leo," I breathe his name out like a dying wish, "this is the most stunning thing I've ever laid my eyes on. Please show me how to use it properly."

"I would love nothing more, Darling." He leans in and gives me a chaste kiss. "Max, would you kindly set up the targets for our wife?"

Nodding, his brother gets to work pulling out wooden posts, each with a bullseye painted on it, along with large taupe sacks covered in small scratches and cuts. Leo moves to assist him with getting everything set.

I sit back in a chair, admiring the way they glisten from the thin layer of sweat that coats their faces. As the last target is positioned exactly where Leo wants it, he turns to me. The impish smirk that pulls at his lips tells me he notices the arousal in my expression.

"Let me show you how to handle that weapon in your hands, then I'll gladly let you handle mine," he purrs, and Guides be damned, it makes my core throb. Max leans on the table across the room, legs crossed and arms folded over, still shirtless, and my already stuttering heart nearly fails altogether.

"It's very unfair that there are two of you, for the record," I huff.

"You appear to enjoy there being two of us when you are between us," Leo retorts.

"Just show me how to use this so we can retire to our bed for the evening." I stand and walk his way, face scrunched.

"I suppose I'll begin dinner preparations then." Max chuckles and leaves the room.

"Well then, it appears we have approximately one hour to cover the basics of wielding a blade." Leo pulls a dagger slightly larger than mine from his waistband. "Concealing your weapon is also of the utmost importance."

"You—"

"Carry this on my person at all times, Darling. You never know when someone may need to meet The Powers Above."

"But there are no weapons in New Promise. Who would ever need to meet your blade?"

"There is one man I can think of at this moment." His hardened eyes fill in the portions he's not saying.

"Leo, I'm not his punching bag any longer. You don't need to worry about Raymond." I place a hand on his shoulder and can feel the tension he holds.

"I will see to it that he is no longer a problem before we depart, and should your mother desire, she can accompany us on our venture."

"She would never. That woman is too proud, too hard-headed to leave this place," I grumble. "I also do not wish to see her again. My whole life, she left me to fend for myself against Raymond. She deserves this misery."

"Very well, on to your lesson." He holds his dagger out before me and demonstrates how to properly grip the handle to ensure I do not slip and harm myself.

Once I understand the proper form, we move on to the sacks, and he has me practice stabbing and slicing the strong, woven fabric. The blade feels fairly natural in my hand, and I could definitely see myself putting it to good use should the need arise.

Satisfied with my progress, Leo helps me secure my dagger before we finish and head up to the kitchen.

Max kisses me on the cheek before handing me a bowl of squash soup. "We'll eat in bed, if you'd still like to spend all night there with us." His eyes shy away from mine, and he bites his lip.

"Maximus Koeler!" I feign shock. "Are you insinuating that I spend the evening with one or both of you inside my various orifices?"

Leo snorts behind me, rounding the counter to grab his own bowl of soup. "May I recommend we eat our dinner out here, then we can bathe together and begin there?"

"Oh, I quite enjoy the sound of that. Would you like to wash my hair tonight, Max?" I ask, moving to take a seat at the table.

"It would be my pleasure, Dearest," he answers brightly and takes his seat.

"So it shall be, my loves." Sipping my soup, I hum in satisfaction at the flavor. "This may just earn you the right to ravage me first tonight."

"I concur." Leo tips his bowl, drinking down the herbaceous goodness before he continues. "This soup is so delicious, you can have her all to yourself. I'll stay out here and gorge myself."

"Leo," I deadpan.

"Okay, fine, I'll join you." He playfully pouts into his bowl, and we all laugh.

The best part of the soup is that it's quick to finish.

We hurry to clean our dishes, and Leo scoops me up and carries me to the bathroom. Max follows and turns the water on before he disrobes.

Bathing together is just the beginning. I fully intend to spend *all* night with them.

Today is a day off from training, thank the Guides. While I do quite enjoy rolling around on top of Max's half-naked body, the soreness is rather annoying. Instead of the padded floor, we're staying in the main room today, skimming through various tomes and journals for more information.

Leo has spent most of his free time here while I learn more grappling techniques. He's confident that we'll find everything we need in the entries.

Max is sprawled out across an old sofa he dragged from the chasm, tome in one hand, glass in the other. "I fear there's nothing more we can learn from these," he says with a huff.

"We mustn't chance overlooking key information," Leo orders. "And do *actually* read the entries, we need to stay diligent."

I giggle into the journal I'm reading, carefully turning the distressed pages. Despite the weathered state, the dates are fairly recent. Apparently, this adventurer had returned to New Promise a mere fifty years ago. As I read through their earlier entries, I'm filled with excitement. One passage in particular catches my eye.

In it are detailed drawings of adorable animals called "dogs". Apparently, they were fierce protectors and loyal companions throughout humanity's history. This adventurer had bonded with one named "Rook".

"I believe I've found something fairly enlightening," I speak up, turning my journal to Leo so that he may read the passage. "It seemed like another ordinary entry for him, detailing his hunting trip with Rook, but the end of this one struck me as odd."

— Anderson Talbot, June 27, 2645

Another successful outing with Rook. He's a natural retriever and does a wonderful job bringing me the birds after I shoot them down. I've nearly mastered this old bow. I often think about the people I left behind. Someday, I will go back and set them free. I've catalogued my experiences so that I may provide proof of life beyond those walls. Perhaps they'll believe me. My time in this place has been wonderful, and I feel everyone must have the opportunity to experience life outside of New Promise. For now, I will focus on building my relationships here. But soon I will make good on my plan and bring this wonderful news to the citizens of New Promise. I can't wait to show them the beauty I've found. To think it's so close to home.

"Wonderful, Darling," Leo praises. "He says sanctuary is close by, so hopefully that means the route I've been drafting is accurate. At this point, it appears we may only need to plan for a one-to-two-day trek. Can you believe that?"

Max sits forward. "Is this sanctuary he promises still there? What if they do not welcome us?"

"Brother, are you feeling well? It's unlike you to question things in such a manner."

"Forgive me, but it is quite literally our lives on the line. I want to ensure we're as prepared and informed as possible," Max deadpans.

"Leo is drafting a genius plan. We'll be fine so long as we're together. Our strongest supports are one another." I walk over and kiss him, climbing into his lap as he leans back on the sofa.

His hands find my hips and squeeze firmly as our kiss deepens. Before we get carried away, I pull back, grabbing his tome to hand it to him. "If you find something helpful, I'll let you take me right here," I murmur, pressing against his erection.

"You're a cruel mistress," he groans. "I quite enjoy it." With a final, chaste kiss, he returns to his journal, holding me in place with his free hand.

"Are you sure you're feeling alright? You're acting much more like Leo and less like Max today." I settle into him as his eyes meet mine over the top of his book.

"In truth, I'm stressed. I apologize if I'm acting too brashly. Your presence is calming, and I would like it if you stayed here with me." His face softens to a more familiar expression. "These past couple of days we've been training, and it has been easier to remove the underlying questions from my mind. Now, sitting here in maddening silence, I have nothing to distract myself. This whisky isn't even proving helpful." He gulps down the last of his amber liquid.

"I apologize, Brother. If you have specific concerns, please voice them. The whisky has helped get me through it... and our nightly intimacy is a reward for staying on task." Leo smirks. "I've been enjoying all of the different things we're trying."

Max presses up into me and grunts. "Please do *not* mention intimacy while our wife is sitting on my erection. Especially if you expect me to be productive."

"Just remind yourself that she's what this is all for. We could have easily stayed here for all our days, never caring about anyone except each other. But we're *us* now. Breaking free from this place is in our best interests."

"You should also have some faith in your brother." I playfully swat his chest. "You know he's the smart one." A laugh bubbles out of me.

"You wound me," he says with a mock gasp. "I suppose that makes me the handsome one."

"We're identical, Maximus," Leo grumbles into the pages he's inspecting.

"You're the sweet one, the funny one." I kiss him quickly. "And the cook. He's the planner, the steady support system when I need it. My reliable foundation. Each of you has your quirks, and I love you just the same."

"Do you ever feel as though we're not enough?" he asks, brows knit together.

"Max," Leo warns, voice flat and low.

I shake my head, having concluded my internal musing.

"It's alright," I reply, looking Max directly in the eyes. "You're so much more than I ever expected. I would not lie about such things and would never cast you aside. With that being said, I—" Inhaling until I fear my lungs may burst, I look between them and exhale, "—I love both of you, and am in this fully. I could potentially feel love for another, who truly knows. However, you're more than enough to convince me that this will work, and it is worth the worry, even death."

Their matching gazes gleam with adoration and excitement. Neither of them moves, likely afraid that they'll scare me away if they do.

"Well, are your worries eased?" I ask Max, turning in his lap so I can sit more comfortably.

He kisses me in response, and I nearly melt under his touch. "You promise?" he asks, hand coming up to frame my face.

Leo steps up to us and kisses me, still firmly in his brother's grasp. He hums as I nibble his lip.

We break apart, and I look between them once more and nod. "I do, I suppose the conversation helped me realize my truth."

Their shoulders relax, bodies appearing lighter and less tense than ever before.

"This is wonderful to hear, Darling." Leo presses his lips to mine a final time before returning to his journal. "We shall show you exactly how much we love you after dinner, but there is still time for more journal entries, and we must stay on track."

Max pulls me into him as I gather my journal and flip to the back few entries and skim through them. It appears that Anderson had a plan, one that clearly did not pan out.

"Leo, look here," I say, holding the journal up as he comes over to us.

— Anderson Talbot October 7, 2645

Tomorrow I begin the venture back to New Promise. The Mayor here and several of the elders have warned me against it. Apparently, years ago, another ex-Promiser attempted the same and never returned. Surely they had a mishap and perished in their travels. I know the way back like a well-worn map. Scouting and hunting all these months have prepared me for the journey. I will be the savior of New Promise. I will show the people the lies. I WILL free them.

"That's troubling, but not entirely surprising. I believe I have the journal of that previous adventurer somewhere. The dates were approximately a decade before Talbot's. Let me see if I can locate it." He returns to the stacks and rustles through them until he spots the one he's looking for. "Yes, here it is. This was from August tenth, twenty-six thirty-two to July ninth of twenty-six thirty-three."

He flips to the last entry, and we gather around.

- Martin Rift, July 9, 2633

Today I embark on the final leg of my journey. New Promise lies just over the next hill. At the present moment, I am unsure what I'll even say once I step foot back inside the gate. The panel on the outside was in my dreams last night, glowing red in warning. Should I heed it and turn back? No, the people must learn the truth. If not me, then no one will.

"So that is two adventurers who definitely returned and were never heard from again?" I ask, eyes wide as my breathing picks up.

"It would appear that way. I'm not sure what the fate of either was, there are no further entries. It seems as though the journals must have been taken by the Guides and banished to the depths of the catacombs, hoping they would never be recovered." Leo takes my hand, squeezing gently to calm my nerves.

"Why not just burn them?" Max questions.

"Likely to avoid speculation. The Guides have electricity. Citizens would likely question them for burning something. There is also the possibility that they wanted to have the information available should they ever need to reference it. Perhaps if things went poorly here, they could use the information in the same manner we are, to find other habitable villages."

"I do not care about this place. If we make it out successfully, promise me that we'll never return." I look at both of them, and they nod in agreement.

"Let us go prepare dinner, Dearest. Today has been tiring, and I'm nearly ready for bed." Max scoops me into his arms, and we begin toward the stairs. "Be ready in an hour, Leo. Don't obsess over it too much."

He closes the journal and stands behind us. "I think I'll join you in dinner preparations. I need to process all the information we've learned today."

I only hope we're learning enough. How can one ever be truly prepared to start a new life in a wasteland?

My body aches from training with Max. I'm learning so many new techniques, but it has been a *very* tiring week. Leo and I are going to the community later today, and I am dreading it. Our small, segmented plot of land feels so far removed from what I once knew. My only desire is to stay *right* here for the rest of my days, securely wrapped in both of their arms.

Leo pulls me into his chest, kissing my forehead as Max presses himself against me, his morning hardness nudging my backside. My core throbs for him, urging me to arch my back. We've taken to sleeping in the nude these past few nights, as my need for them has been unyielding. Something about rolling around on the padded floor of our training room has ignited a raging fire in my loins.

I shift slightly again until his length can slip between my thighs. Rumbles escape his chest as he stirs. When he presses his hips forward, I moan his name.

Leo trails a hand up my chest and takes hold of my jaw, bringing our mouths together as I work against his brother. The friction of Max's manhood against my tingling clit nearly drives me to insanity.

As I whimper, Leo pulls his lips from mine, eyes focusing on Max. "Don't be a tease. You know what she wants," he commands before slipping his tongue into my mouth. I gasp as Max thrusts into me in one fluid motion.

"Beautiful," Leo says against my lips. "Absolute perfection." His hips move, prodding my stomach with his erection. I take hold of him, working him in my palm as Max lazily moves inside me.

"Let me taste you," I plead.

He stands from the bed, and Max pulls out of me just long enough to allow for repositioning. Leo sits against the headboard, and I settle on my knees before him, stroking his length a few times as I run my tongue just under the skin that conceals the head of his member.

Max takes his place behind me and bottoms out, plunging deeper than ever. I sputter and moan around Leo as the sudden sensation causes waves of pleasure to course through my veins. He thrusts into my mouth, hitting the back of my throat until I choke on him.

Max drives himself into me faster, harder, as he nears his release—his hand sliding around to stroke my sensitive clit.

"That's it, Darling, take what you need from us whenever it pleases you," Leo groans, hand tightening in my hair as I bob up and down around him, hissing as his release nears. The force of Max slamming into me only drives Leo deeper into my throat as he bursts. With a roar, he holds me in place, hips jerking as the last waves of his orgasm hit.

Max increases the speed of his circles on my clit, and my screams of pleasure get muffled by Leo's manhood until I collapse between them.

Leo finally slips out of my mouth, and I gasp for air, giving him a drunken smile. He runs his fingers across my cheeks, wiping away my tears, as Max adjusts his angle. With a few deep pumps, he grips my backside, overcome by the force of his orgasm.

His shuddering thrusts stimulate the perfect spot, bringing me a sudden second climax. I tighten around him and he groans, gripping me tighter as we ride the waves of pleasure together.

The three of us lay here savoring each other's affectionate touches before Max steps away to grab a rag for me. I rest my head on Leo's lap as he runs his fingers through my hair while we wait for him to return.

"You're such a gift, Phoebe." Leo's voice is faint, as if he's afraid he'll scare me away.

I roll slightly to turn my head and meet his eyes. "You've given me a life worth living, both of you." I turn my attention to Max as he enters the room, a gentle smile on my face. "I apologize for my skepticism in the beginning, but I am serious. I'll go wherever you do, even if that means death."

"It won't," Leo assures me. "But we do have to make a trip to the community today, despite our distraction this morning. There are necessary preparations that must be handled prior to our departure."

"I'm aware," I groan and roll my eyes. Max chuckles from his place between my legs as he tidies up the mess he's made.

"Keep laughing, I'll make you do it," Leo threatens with a soft chuckle. "I despise dealing with the old farmer as much as you do. But we cannot leave the hens unattended after we leave, and we have no way to take them with us."

Right, the hens.

My lips pull into a pout as reality creeps in.

"Speak your troubles, Dearest," Max says as he takes a seat next to Leo.

"I've only now realized that, aside from training and the few helpful entries I've found, I know nothing of the escape plan." I sit up and address them directly. "I do not appreciate being kept in the dark when my safety is a concern."

"Darling, I apologize for not detailing our plan to you. I suppose in the process of preparing you to fend for yourself, we've overlooked the finer details. Let us get done with the farmer, and we shall discuss the plan over dinner. Is that acceptable?"

"I would appreciate that. Thank you, Leo." I nod and stand to grab a tunic.

"Shall I make breakfast before you depart? I know your errands will take some time. I would hate to have you hungry." Max rises to his feet and joins me at the closet, finding a pair of slacks that suit him.

I tie my tunic closed and rise onto my toes to kiss him. He wraps me up and lifts me off the ground as our mouths meet. Giggling as he places me back onto my feet, I look up at him and smile. "That would be wonderful, my love."

"Would you care to join me?" he asks, as if I would ever pass up the opportunity to cook with him. It has become one of my favorite activities.

The air is cooler today than it has been, I believe it is nearly November. We don't have weather like the history books outline, but the temperature still shifts around this time of year. I trudge along beside Leo with his hand on the small of my back as we enter the heart of the community. I had nearly forgotten how loud it can be here since the meeting. The surrounding crowds nearly drown out the sounds of our flock in the wagon he's towing.

Fortunately, this should be my last time coming here. While I do not know the details, I am fully aware that we plan to leave before the next meeting in a week's time.

The dusty streets bustle with people—primarily men—going about their day. Trading for goods, discussing their duties, sharing stories of their sons, never their daughters. The further we venture, the more I'm reminded of the reasons I'm willing to risk it all. Factually, I know I should question my morality for being alright leaving and forgetting all about this place, but I do not.

Everyone here lives in a blissful state of ignorance, none the wiser that the lives they're living are fabricated lies built meticulously over time to maintain the Guides' control over their kingdom—no matter how small it may be.

Leo and Max have told me stories from long ago about "great leaders" who were actually deceitful, and I never understood how they came to power. I still don't, but seeing the generational effects laid out before me is nauseating. Regardless of *how* New Promise came to be, the continued following that the Guides have is astonishing.

All of these men, given everything they need *and* the unyielding loyalty of a woman just so she can guarantee her survival, and for what? What is the point of any of this, except for those in charge to continue their reign?

Pathetic.

"Darling." Leo's hand flexes against my back. "You're scowling something fierce, people are taking notice."

"Oh, my apologies." I drift my gaze to the stone pathway we're traveling and bite my lip.

"Do not worry, I interrupted to make you aware. We're nearly at the farm. Once there, it should be a fairly quick transaction. I'll return the hens he's lent us and thank him for his grace with some parchments for his walls."

"That is all it takes? How long have you had the hens?" I nearly look him in the eye before remembering my etiquette training. A familiar dullness pulls at the back of my mind.

"We traditionally keep them for a couple of years, until they stop laying their eggs, at which point I believe he trades them to the rations manager for extra ingredients. Did your family never trade?"

"No, my father has nothing of value..."

"Right, that explains his willingness to accept my proposal." He chuckles. "Best deal of my life. A silly pillow for the perfect woman." He rubs my back.

"A pillow," I scoff. "I still can not believe the foolishness. What is he to do with a *pillow*?"

"He can suffocate himself with it for all I care." Disdain drips from his words.

"You truly want to end him, but why?"

"He hurt you. That is all the reason I need."

I look at him and take note of the harsh lines caused by the deep frown he's wearing. Strangely, I feel a slight pang of excitement at the thought of him putting an end to my father. I'm nearly giddy, suppressing a smile as we approach the farm.

"Ah, Leo, nice to see you. To what do I owe the pleasure?" The rotund older man has a sickeningly fake smile on his face. "Here to trade your wife for my daughter?" A boisterous laugh bursts out of him.

Bite your tongue, Phoebe.

Marrying your daughter off to a historian is a status symbol. Next to the Guides, they're the most revered and respected members of New Promise. Fortunately, I landed in the arms of the good ones.

"Simon, I would like to return the flock of hens, nothing more. I'm absolutely satisfied with my wife, thank you." He uncovers the wagon, and I watch Simon's face shift to one of confusion.

That is, until he spots the mountain of parchments Leo brought in return.

"Wonderful, I hope they were to your liking and supplied you with a sufficient amount of eggs. Are you in need of something else to replace them?" Grabbing two hens per hand, he carries them to the pen near his home. "I have a sow about to birth new piglets."

"At this moment, I'm not interested. I shall let you know when I'm ready for more. They did well for me." Leo nods and covers the wagon back up once they've all been moved. "Thank you again, please enjoy the parchments."

As we make our way back toward the heart of New Promise, Leo takes me by surprise. He ushers me to a shop, and I rear my head back. "What is the meaning of this detour?" I ask.

"I want to do something nice for you. Your hair is getting long and unruly. How would you like a trim? You can have it styled however you like."

A haircut? I don't know that I've ever had one, aside from the ones given to us during training. If you can call them that.

"I've always wanted bangs, the type that go across my forehead. Would that be acceptable?" I ask quietly, eyes darting toward one of the barber's chairs.

We're in the far corner of the shop, but the red-haired man across the way catches my eye. Prime Guide Ogden's guard is here, off-duty, getting his hair touched up.

His eyes lock with mine, and I'm unable to look away. I'm unsure why he watches me like this every time he has an opportunity. His face is always impassive, but the emotions his eyes give away are confusing. His gaze almost feels as though he yearns for a connection like the one I share with Leo.

I know nothing of the guards or what they do beyond their duties. However, the rumors state that they're womanizers, never settling for a wife.

"I think bangs would look wonderful, Darling," Leo answers, oblivious to the silent confusion I'm suffering through.

As the barber approaches, he greets Leo and asks for the specifications he's looking for. I remember rule five—never make eye contact with a married man—and keep my gaze lowered.

Seconds later, I get careless and let my attention wander back to the guard as Leo talks to the man chopping away at my hair. I could swear his pale cheeks flush, but surely it has nothing to do with me. Looking his way feels illicit, like this is a test. But a sensation simmers just below the surface of my skin. An unfamiliar prickle of interest.

If word gets back to the Guides, they could try to make Leo execute me for this. I tremble and bring my attention back to my lap, cursing my curiosity. Such a mishap might have cost us everything.

Foolish, Phoebe.

I shake off the negative emotions as the barber finishes, and Leo trades him a tapestry.

We begin our return home. My stomach rumbles the closer we get to our dwelling, eager to devour whatever delicious meal Max has prepared for us. Today's visit to the community was less eventful than I had expected until I likely ruined it by ogling another man.

Perhaps nothing will come of it, but life loves to remind me of where I came from.

Just as it does now.

As we approach the hedge where our dwelling sits, none other than Raymond Harding calls out to us, sporting the same furious expression that still attempts to infiltrate even my loveliest of dreams.

"You've robbed me, boy," he spits, marching toward us menacingly. "She's worth so much more than a pathetic pillow, and I've come to reclaim her."

"How did you know where to find us?" Leo steps in front of me.

"Silly boy, the Guides know where you live." Raymond rolls his eyes with a curled lip. "Now give me back what you stole."

My knees buckle, and I drop to the ground, unable to bite back the panic setting in.

This is it. I'm about to go back to a life of misery.

"You accepted my trade," Leo says, voice flat.

"Well, I'm unaccepting it. The Guides said there's a three-month rule. If either side is unhappy, the marriage is off. And I ain't happy. Found someone better, willing to trade something fancier." His face splits into a nightmare-inducing half-toothless grin.

"I'm going to have to insist that you leave." Leo reaches behind his back, standing tall.

Breathing becomes impossible as I struggle to stay conscious.

All the progress, all the things I've learned, I cannot go back.

"Th-the b-b-button," I choke out, begging Leo to end this, end me. "I c-can't." Black spots fill my vision.

"Don't you dare press her button to get outta this, it would be the end of you, Koeler. Murdering a woman who no longer belongs to you is a banishable offense." Raymond stalks closer, pure evil in his eyes.

Leo goes stiff. "Last chance to walk away." He glances over his shoulder at me with a terrifying gleam in his eye.

He might actually do it. I think I'm about to die.

Everything around us stands still as Raymond marches forward. Leo reaches into his waistband, and I prepare for death. Only, I've been so distracted by my emotional distress that I've forgotten one key factor. Leo doesn't carry a button... he carries a dagger.

In a flash, he unsheathes his blade, meeting Raymond mid-stride and impaling him with practiced finesse. Gurgling noises are all I can hear as Leo stands with his blade buried in Raymond's stomach. My held breath rushes out in force, speeding up as Leo turns his hardened gaze to me. It softens the slightest amount as our eyes meet, before redirecting his attention to the man doubled over in front of him.

"You will *never* harm her again. This has been a long time coming, and I had feared I would never get the pleasure of watching the life fade from your eyes," he sneers, twisting the dagger deeper as Raymond wails. "Go on, scream. Beg for mercy, just as Phoebe has done to you numerous times over. The difference is that I'm doing this out of love for her. And the best part." He leans back, lifting Raymond's face to look him in the eye. "Nobody will *ever* find your remains."

I gasp as he removes the blade and drives it back in, unnaturally mesmerized by the display. My panic dies as Raymond does, heartbeat slowing, breaths regulating.

He did it.

I look at Leo and wish I could speak, but I am too smitten, too enraptured.

"Darling, please bring the wagon in. I need to handle the refuse." He hoists the small frame of my now-lifeless father over his shoulders and moves through the hedge.

I'm left just outside, speechless and inexplicably hungry for him. Did I think he was serious about the threats? Surely. But I, too, had never imagined a situation arising where he'd be able to make good on them. Mere seconds were all it took, and surely that is because Leo *wanted* it to take that long. He made sure Raymond knew exactly why he was meeting his fate.

Right, the wagon.

I shuffle to get back into the safety of our property, ensuring there's no trace of blood near the entrance. Once the wagon is in place, I swing open the hatch and nearly stumble on the tricky upper landing. The steps have never felt so long, so ominous, before now. As I reach the main room, there's nothing but silence to greet me. Everything feels normal. It's as if I didn't just witness a murder. The only thing out of place in the slightest is that neither of my husbands is here to greet me.

A faint trail of blood, only a few stray drops every few footsteps, catches my eye, directing me where to go. Naturally, it leads to the study. Simple problem-solving skills tell me they must be securing his remains deep within the catacombs. Leo has clearly thought this through.

Should I feel remorse? Guilt? Sadness? Any emotion at all? I'm not sure.

As I come to the bottom of the lengthy staircase leading to the catacombs, I follow the trail through the large chambers until I see them. Max and a blood-soaked Leo are standing over Raymond's body, talking quietly. They stop when I get close enough to notice, Leo's face filled with a tumultuous expression. It appears that he thinks I may be upset.

"Darling, I—" he begins to apologize, but I jump into his arms and kiss him deeply. As I lace my hands through his hair, he turns and pins me against the wall, nipping at my neck.

"I told you she would not be upset." Max chuckles.

I moan as Leo's hands grasp my backside. "Come here, Max. I need both of you."

He wastes no time stepping to take me from Leo so that he may remove his soiled shirt.

"Your tunic is bloody now," Max says, untying the sash at my waist. "I suppose it will have to go."

In seconds, we're all fully nude, aching, and fueled by adrenaline. I drop to my knees and take Leo into my mouth, and he gasps.

"Guides mercy, do you have anyone else we can end if this is the reward?" Max asks as he kneels and lines himself up behind me.

He drives in deep, giving me all he has, and I wail around Leo.

"Powers Above, you're filthy," he growls, pulling my hair.

They slam into me from both sides, taking me with the intensity I crave, showing no mercy. This is raw and explosive. Nothing about the way our bodies are melding together is intimate, nor can it be labeled as purely intercourse. This is *sex*. Rough, emotional, feral.

My fingernails dig into Leo's thighs as he nears release, cursing my name to the skies. Max inserts his thumb into my back entrance while he erupts inside me, helping me plummet into the abyss of ecstasy.

"Swallow him," Max grits out, slamming into me. And I do.

Leo uses his grip on my hair to angle my throat perfectly, so that he may bury himself as he spills his release. I peer up at his face as he lets go, blood smeared and blissed-out. Beauty and carnage bundled in a perfect package.

As we all pant and regain our sanity, I let out a laugh.

There is no way The Powers Above would approve of this.

Bathing has never been so warranted. The three of us emerge from the catacombs coated in blood and an amalgamation of our own bodily fluids.

If my soul was not already destined for an eternity of damnation for bedding two men at once, it will be now. Surely the ancient texts have a law against fornication next to the corpse of your dead father, whom your husband murdered in your name, no less. Soul be damned, I will never show remorse for Raymond Harding, and the sexual encounter that arose from all of that adrenaline was phenomenal.

As the water warms, Max steps up behind me and wraps me in his arms, kissing my cheek. "You were fantastic, as always." Burying his face in the crook of my neck, he inhales. "I love you, Dearest."

"And I love you, Maximus," I reply instantly, no longer needing to consider my feelings. "I love you too, Leonidas." I turn to him as he enters, upper body still smeared with blood.

He says nothing, just kisses me while I'm securely wrapped in his brother's embrace. Few things make me feel as though I'm melting, but moments like this do it every time.

We step into the shower chamber, and the overhead spray begins rinsing away the evidence of our afternoon escapades. Gathering soap on a rag, I scrub Leo's chest, leaning in to steal a kiss along the way. Max waits his turn, claiming my lips as I help him wash up.

Together they run their hands along every curve of my body, ensuring I'm thoroughly rinsed before we turn the water off.

We quickly dry ourselves and head to the kitchen to make dinner.

"This is the last of our squash, Dearest. Fortunately, we'll only be here a couple more days. I'll make it my mission to locate some as soon as I'm able to." Max cubes the orange-fleshed vegetable and tosses it into a pan. "Would you be so kind as to prepare the herbs?"

I nod and get to work chopping a variety of small green leaves. We work in a calm silence as Leo sets the table.

"We also have just enough meat for two more days. Looks like the plan will be ready before we know it," Leo speaks up. "I will pack the rations tonight to ensure they're ready. I'll have the wagon prepared by morning, then we just need to ensure our affairs are all in order by the time we're good to go. November will be the beginning of our new lives."

"Oh, I was right then! I had noticed how cool it was and assumed November was near." I beam at him.

"Yes, Darling, you are correct. From November on, we will be free of this place." He smiles back at me as Max finishes the last touches on our dinner.

We move to the table, dishing out our portions as we take our seats. I wait patiently, nibbling at my food, anticipating the moment one of them speaks. Chewing the flavorful meat and mashed squash, I look between them.

"Okay," Leo says with a faint laugh, "I've made you wait long enough. I wish this plan were better thought out. However, I do not believe that getting banished will be a difficult task." Pausing, he wipes his mouth.

Max picks up where he left off, "We're simply going to expose ourselves." He leans back in his chair. "There is, obviously, more to it than that. But in short, that is the plan. We'll go in two days, with our loaded wagon, and instead of the town meeting, we will show the Guides our best-kept secret... me."

"*That* is the plan? You feel as though being twins is an offense worthy of banishment?" I scrunch my face up and shake my head.

"Darling, I believe you underestimate how strictly the Guides enforce the laws laid out by The Powers Above. Our parents were a perfect example. They did no harm to anyone, but since they did not conform to patriarchal ideologies, they were banished. For merely daring to love one another." Leo takes my hand, squeezing softly. "It may seem foolish, however, I fully believe this is what will occur the instant our truth comes to light."

"And if they do not?" I look between them.

"Then we fight our way out. I nearly got banished for punching one guard. Imagine if we go after the entire force? None of them have any formal training; they're merely large in frame, an intimidation tactic." Max takes my other hand and smiles.

"Speaking of guards..." I chew my lip, unsure of how to proceed. "The redhead who is Prime Guide's personal detail seems to have a fascination with me. Or perhaps I'm the one enchanted. Regardless, I may have compromised our plan by staring at him while we got our hair cut earlier."

"Darling, are you attracted to him?" Leo tilts his head, single brow quirked.

"I do not know," I say to the table.

"Attraction is nothing to be ashamed of. We appreciate your honesty. If you ever find a man who appeals to you, we would welcome him openly. So long as he is respectful, right, Max?" Leo looks across the table.

"Absolutely, however, a guard may not prove the wisest choice, my love." He chuckles.

"Guides no." I giggle in return. "Surely the guards have access to the unwed concubines and would know nothing about how to be a husband of your caliber."

"Regardless, your honesty is precious and ap-preciated. Now, finish your dinner. We'll get to work on packing tunics and spare goods. There's not much I can imagine we'll require for our journey, but it would be wise to prepare for the worst," Leo says.

"Few things are worse than death, my love," I offer in return.

As we clear the table, Leo gathers rations and canteens to load into the wagon while Max and I get to work packing the bedroom. Our closet is the first to go. We exchange excited smiles and soft kisses in passing, despite the melancholy reason for our packing, we enjoy the process.

I gather some trinkets from the study that I find appealing and include some of Leo's favorite tomes—making sure to pack the love story we're in the middle of reading. Everything is coming together, and while I do not know how well the plan will work, I am excited to see what comes of it. Fighting a couple of guards also sounds invigorating.

Once the last of our bedroom is packed, except for a couple of spare tunics, Max and I collapse onto the bed. I roll over to my side and lay my head on his chest as we wait for Leo to return from his wagon packing duties.

"It's all going to be worth it in the end, Dearest," Max murmurs as he twirls my hair around his finger. "We will be together, nothing will stop us."

I hum in contentment as we lay in a peaceful silence.

Footsteps slam against the floor, barreling down the hallway, and Leo bursts into the room with a frenzied look on his face. "Prime Guide Ogden is on his way with his guard. Max, hide in the closet. Phoebe, stay here."

"What?!" I freeze in place as Leo sprints back down the hall.

Max kisses me on the cheek, but I can't respond. I can't process any of the sensations going through my body. He says something I can't hear and slips into the closet as my heart threatens to burst out of my body.

I stay in place, sitting on the bed as voices sound from down the hall. Try as I might, I'm not quite able to hear the words being said. The urge to run burns like fire under my feet as they grow closer.

Is he here to question Leo? Surely Raymond is not missed already. But perhaps my mother reported him absent from dinner. If so, why would they come here of all places? How am I supposed to help?

Prime Guide Ogden sneers as he enters the room. "I am here to inform your husband that you're being reclaimed. We sent your father, but it would appear he never returned."

I give Leo a look of desperation, unable to speak.

Standing just behind the Prime Guide, I watch as his guard's face falls, warring with himself.

"I'm afraid I still don't understand," Leo speaks up, stepping next to me.

"It's simple, we should never have allowed you to marry her. She's to be with a man who can properly control her behavior, not one who consistently allows her to misbehave in public and defy The Powers Above." By the victorious look on his face, he knows that Leo is already blaming himself; the defeat is apparent. "Your father fell victim to a salacious vixen as well, using her sexual manipulation to fool him into going against the law."

"So, what is the process then?" Leo asks.

"Glad you asked. We'll take her today, spend tomorrow deciding her fate, and then remarry her if she passes her training exams." He has the audacity to smile as the words fall from his venomous tongue.

"So this is why you've brought a guard? To ensure you've got me outnumbered, should I try to resist?" Leo asks, voice cold and flat.

"No, it is protection in case she were to try anything nefarious. You're an upstanding citizen." A soft snort rushes out of Leo, and Prime Guide Ogden tilts his head. "Do you disagree?"

"I just have two questions, Highness. When citizens are banished, is it done publicly? Who handles the banishing?"

"Are you suggesting you would defy an order from The Powers Above and face banishment?"

"Who. Handles. The. Banishing?" His breathing grows frenzied, control on the brink of snapping as the clipped words fire out of his mouth.

"The guards are the ones who protect the code to the gate and handle the banishing duties. It would be unbecoming of the Guides. We also do not make a spectacle, as banishment can be quite a melancholy event." He steps back behind his guard as Leo's eyes harden.

More melancholy than execution? Is he mad?

"Well, then." Leo stands straight, looking between Prime Guide Ogden and the young man standing between us. "I know which of the two will live to see tomorrow. Max."

As Prime Guide Ogden opens his mouth to question Leo, the closet doors swing apart, and I see nothing more than Max's hands on either side of his head as it swivels. The cracking of his neck echoes through the room, followed by a thud as his body falls to the ground.

Before the guard can react, Leo pounces, securing his hands behind him with a tunic sash.

"This just got rather complicated." Leo huffs.

Complicated is an understatement.

Max stands over Prime Guide Ogden's body, eyes cold, as I approach him. He shifts his attention to me, and I watch as his casual, light-hearted expression returns. When I rest my hands on his shoulders, he scoops me up into a loving embrace. As he squeezes, I grunt and laugh softly, kissing him as he loosens his grip.

"What have you done?" the guard wails as he struggles against his restraints. "What will you do with me and what of his body?"

"He can rot alongside Raymond," Leo quips, leaning toward him. "Fortunately for you, you're too valuable to die... yet."

"I'm as good as dead either way. They'll banish me for failing my duties," he sputters around the tears streaming down his face. "Do you understand that you've already killed me?"

My chest aches for him. The defeat and self-criticism in his expression draw me in. Realistically, he's done nothing wrong, aside from existing in this world. Surely, like the rest of us, he had no say in his job assignment. Now he'll likely pay for that misfortune with his life. I curl closer into Max, eyes affixed to the guard.

Watching them kill Raymond and Prime Guide Ogden was exhilarating. Each of them was a horrible evil, casting a dark shroud over my life. They deserved death. But this man? His presence, his very energy as it shakes up the room, is not malicious.

I swallow, holding back my sudden upset at the thought of Leo killing him when the time comes. It does not give me the same thrill; my chest tightens, and I must divert my attention for fear of crying.

Leo stands to his full height and folds his arms over, still addressing the guard, "Perhaps banishment won't be as cruel as you assume. You could always leave with us. You're young, muscular, and surely could be an extra pair of hands at the least."

My breath is trapped in my lungs from his words. Flutters bounce around in my stomach as I look at Leo and find sincerity in his expression. I should not be surprised, he's not a cold-blooded killer, and surely can also sense that this man is not deserving of death.

Max shoots him a questioning look. "And what if he betrays us? Far be it from me to ask the logical questions, but surely he cannot be trusted."

"What difference would it make?" our red-haired prisoner asks, face filled with devastation. "We'll all perish in days. Starvation is slow and agonizing."

No longer able to resist, I slip out of Max's hold and kneel before him, caught off guard by his strong, chiseled features. Seeing them this close-up has my breath stuck in my throat. "What is your name?" I keep my voice soft, attempting to calm his troubled mind.

"Kole," he breathes out, deep blue eyes meeting mine. "I-I do not wish to die. I've barely begun my life." He trembles, sniffing back the last of his initial upset.

"What if I share some information with you? I don't wish for you to be afraid." I lay my hand on his shoulder and he flinches at first, but breathes deep and leans into my touch.

"They just murdered the Prime Guide in front of me..." His eyes dance between my men, strong jaw working back and forth.

"He deserved it. The way he spoke of our wife was abhorrent," Leo states, voice measured but not unkind.

"You killed... for her?" He looks to Max, face twisted as he blinks rapidly. He appears to be lost in thought, contemplative.

"He came here to take her away," Max answers, as if the explanation makes perfect sense to anyone aside from us.

I watch as Kole looks between them again, realization overtaking his face as he finally takes notice of his full situation. "Why are there two of you?" He leans back against the wall, finding a slight bit of comfort. "You're nearly the same. What is this trickery?"

"No tricks, just a well-kept secret. We mean you no harm, but do know that our wife comes first above all others." Leo steps beside me and kneels. "May you know the love of a beautiful woman someday and understand."

"Love? We do not love anymore, it goes against the laws of The Powers Above," he proclaims, though it's not as sure as I would expect. Max takes my other side as Kole continues, "Love is viewed as a weakness, preventing men from meeting their full potential. Love makes people careless."

"Love has made me brave. Their love has shown me kindness I've never known, and has brought me enjoyment I never thought possible." I lean into Leo as Max places a hand on my knee. "I was hesitant at first, but now that I have it, I never want to be without it."

"I..." His chest deflates. "What I believe is of no importance. I'm merely a failed guard, three months into the job, and I've let the Prime Guide be murdered." He looks over to the body lying lifeless behind us. "He was a cruel man. I will not mourn him. Unfortunately, his son is no different. Mikael has been eagerly awaiting the day he gets to claim his father's throne."

Leo shifts me into Max's lap and stands. "You two keep our guest occupied, I shall take care of the body. Do be careful." He leaves the room, huffing under the weight of Prime Guide Ogden draped over his shoulders.

Max holds me securely against him, fingers combing through my hair. I lay my head against his chest and hum in appreciation. With my eyes closed, I can still sense Kole's attention, focused intently on us.

Moments pass in silence, and I nearly fall asleep before Max leans against the bed, repositioning me in his lap. He cups my cheek, kissing me softly and I whimper with need.

"Not now, Dearest, we have an audience." Max chuckles."I don't think Kole would appreciate the show."

I'm so entranced by Max that I forget about our situation. Across from us, still leaning against the wall, Kole's blue eyes slowly travel the length of my body, intense as every other time I've been in his presence. He swallows hard and licks his lower lip as I turn to face him.

"Do you... please both of them?" His question comes out rough.

"She does," Max answers, pulling me against him. "We also ensure she is *thoroughly* pleased." He rests his chin on my shoulder and locks his hands together around my waist.

"*You* please *her*?" Kole sits up straighter, head tilted with his question.

"Indeed, the sensation is far better than anything I can describe. I highly recommend giving it a try." Max squeezes me gently with a soft chuckle.

"W-with her?" Kole's face flushes, and I bite back a grin at the confirmation that I have not imagined his fascination with me.

"What? I-uh," Max stammers behind me. "I... had not intended to suggest you please Phoebe. But, should she wish for it, I would not be opposed. Though I cannot speak for Leo."

I jerk my head back, turning to face Max. "You... you would allow another man to please me?"

"What?" Leo asks from the doorway, startling the three of us. His stare pierces Kole, face tight.

"I was not attempting to seduce your wife, Leo. I would not know the first thing about pleasing a woman." His face falls as he shuffles to adjust his arms. "Though the concept is intriguing, and she is beautiful."

"I had merely forgotten he was present and was lost in Max's affection, nothing more." I offer a warm smile to Leo as he sits next to us.

"Not to worry, Darling. You may find your pleasure where you wish, so long as we are not forgotten." He kisses me with an unyielding amount of pressure, hand falling to my hip. A breathless moan escapes me as he pulls away, my attention focused solely on him. "Now, shall we retire for the evening? I'm quite drained from the day."

"What of me?" Kole asks, face pained. "If I may make one request, to have my wrists bound in front of me so that I may sleep more comfortably?" Gentle and honest, his tear-stung eyes beg for our compassion.

Consider me too kind for my own good, because I turn to Leo, jutting my lower lip out. "I trust that he will not harm us. Please let him find some comfort."

"You do have a soft spot for the guard, after all." His voice is light, expression slightly quizzical as he chuckles.

"I am not entirely sure how to respond." I tuck my chin to my chest, shrinking into myself. "He is attractive in his own right, and we've shared glances, as I've stated. I am drawn to him."

Leo brushes my bangs back and presses his lips to my forehead, a soft smile on his face as he pulls away. "Because it will please Phoebe, and you've shown no ill will, you may share our bed on the far side of Max. This way, any attempt you make to flee in the night will alert all of us."

"Fleeing and returning without the Prime Guide would be death. You have secured that fate for me regardless. I may as well remain on the side with the potential to keep me alive. I swear to bring no harm to you." He bows his head and Leo helps him to his feet.

Once his wrists are unbound, he shakes his shoulders and rolls his neck, then holds his arms out to be retied. Shocking us all, Leo tosses the binding to the side and tips his head toward the bed. "This is careless, but something leads me to believe you speak the truth. Do not make me regret this decision."

Max and I take our places in the center, and I rest my head on his chest. Awkwardly, Kole circles us and lies next to Max. Leo curls himself around me, gently kissing my shoulder as Max kisses the top of my head. I spare stray glances at Kole as they fawn over me. Any other night, we would please each other until sleep welcomes us.

Now, I'm left wondering about the red-haired stranger in our bed.

As my husbands drift off to sleep, I lie awake observing Kole—still, silent, rigid. He jolts as I reach across Max and touch his defined bicep. "My apologies, I did not intend to startle you." I keep my voice hushed to avoid waking the others as I trace a vein bulging on his forearm. Max and Leo are strong, but Kole is more physically imposing. I've not been in the presence of a man of his stature before.

He turns his head toward me, cataloging my position—securely wrapped in the arms of my men. "What drove them to love you?" he asks, gaze drifting to my finger as it trails a faint path along his skin.

"Oh, they loved me before I was brought here." I chuckle softly. "It was me who needed convincing." Leo pulls me closer and nuzzles against my shoulder.

"They're... at ease." Kole's brows pinch together. "I do not know the last time I slept as peacefully."

"You could right now if you'd only relax. No harm will come to you so long as you don't threaten me." I give him a faint smile, hoping he's able to see it in the dim light.

"I wouldn't dream of such a thing. Despite my job assignment, I'm not a violent man." He swallows hard, eyes soft as he addresses me.

"Aside from the tension and original outburst, you're surprisingly calm for someone who witnessed a murder mere hours ago." I raise a brow.

"As are you," he retorts, a single eyebrow lifting to mirror my expression.

"The murder was to *protect* me. It was quite literally a life-or-death situation. Prime Guide Ogden was also very cruel to me, and I do not mourn him," I respond with a no-nonsense tone.

"His words were poorly chosen today, and he made our coming here sound much more nefarious than needed. However, knowing how your men love you, it would have been a painful goodbye." His eyes go distant for a moment before he blinks it away. "Prime Guide was unkind on his best days. The heinous acts I had to witness were beyond worthy of death."

"Is that why you're unwed? I notice many of the guards marry late in life, if at all." Much to my pleasure, my curiosity doesn't seem to offend him.

"I wanted a bride, someone I could cherish behind closed doors. A woman who would let me express my abnormal feelings without fear of her telling the Guides. I, too, believe in love and compassion, as unlikely as that may be. However, I know nothing about how to please a woman, nor would I have had the time to learn," he grumbles, a frown pulling at his lips.

"You have no clue what you've missed out on," Leo speaks groggily behind me, causing a breathy laugh to leave my nose.

"What is it like being pleased by another?" Kole rolls to his side, resting his head on his hand.

His interest sparks tiny jolts of excitement in me. My body itches to show him.

"It's not about *being* pleased. The sensation of sharing pleasure with someone you feel deeply for is invigorating and rewarding. Even when I merely watch as Phoebe and Max please one another. Her enjoyment is paramount. May you understand someday."

"If I live past tomorrow," he responds.

"If you choose to join us, you'll survive and live to see a world you've never known. We are not monsters, and would gladly accept you." Leo stretches behind me.

"I have no choice but to accompany you. How many times must I repeat myself?" Kole snips, immediately biting his lip.

Max stirs below my cheek, turning his head to face Kole. "Please stop yelling in my ear before I make Leo sleep between us. He *will* cuddle you and make you even more uncomfortable."

Leo scoffs and a soft snort escapes me. "Max is not lying. Leo is a natural cuddler."

"Powers Above," Kole groans as he rolls onto his back, tossing an arm over his face. "How am I meant to survive with the likes of you?"

"Do, or do not; your cooperation is only required to get us free. Beyond the gate, you may go your own way. It makes no difference to me," Leo says with a sleep-roughened voice just as he yawns and dozes back off.

"They're extremely compassionate men if you give them the opportunity to care," I reassure him just above a whisper.

"Yes, if you're their wife and not another man whom she keeps giving her attention to. I've seen women executed for less." Kole's voice takes on a somber tone.

Max grumbles and moves me over to the other side of him, placing me between his body and Kole's. I squeak as he turns me toward our hesitant ally. "Kiss him or something. Do what you must. I do not care if you please one another right here, so long as you're *quiet.*"

"I second that. Guide's mercy, some of us are trying to sleep. We do not care so long as you're not trying to steal her away," Leo speaks up before rolling to his opposite side.

"I apologize for their brashness," I whisper, looking into Kole's vibrant eyes, like slivers of moonlight on the water in the dimly lit room. "Allow me a moment and I'll move back between them."

His hand that is pinned beneath me curls to encircle my waist, stopping to rest on my hip. Gently, he squeezes, meeting my gaze. "You're warm. Warmer than I had imagined." He inhales a shaky breath. "And soft." Another faint knead of my flesh.

"I would be rather concerned if the opposites were true." I hold back a laugh. "You are warm as well." And he is. His embrace is welcoming. I'm eager for more, in ways I would have never anticipated mere months ago.

Encouraged by his undivided attention, I trail my fingers along his chest, admiring the firmness.

His gaze falls to his nether regions for a second, noticeably hard, and back to my face, eyes widened. "I-I must apologize for my reaction. I've never been in such close quarters with someone so beautiful before. Today has been wildly confusing and you're a married woman, please do not be offended."

"It is a natural occurrence, no need to apologize. Neither of my husbands had been this close with a woman before me, either," I whisper, keeping our gazes locked. "And my touch still garners the same reaction from them."

"And yet they know how to please you. How? We are not taught to seek a woman's pleasure." Breathy and dry, his words are filled with an eagerness I find endearing.

"They studied some of the tomes they possess. Most of it was learned in the moment." I smile softly. "Perhaps we will find other women on our travels, then you may have the chance to feel love for one."

"You believe that other humans have survived?" His fingertips trail lazily across my skin, feeling natural and intentional. Our bodies have come to an understanding that our minds are still unsure of.

"The journals we've read outline whole communities, not just stray settlements. We have to believe it to be true," I whisper, "It would seem that the Guides have maintained a false truth for the sake of their own hubris."

"Would you help me?" He pulls in a sharp breath and clears his throat. "Disregard that." Unsure of his meaning, I slide my hand below the covers, trailing toward his erection. He doesn't stop me at first, lying with his lips slightly parted.

As I nearly make contact, he speaks up, "I did not mean with that."

I go still as he closes his eyes and sighs. "I... misunderstood. I-I thought you wanted me to please you." Dejected, my throat feels tight as I swallow.

"I want pleasure, yes. But what I had meant to ask is for your assistance in learning how to love a woman. Perhaps Max and Leo would be better suited."

"Oh, I'm sure we can all be of assistance." Giving in to my desire, I grip him securely in my hand. He gasps, fingers finding purchase on my hip.

"Y-you don't need to do this. I did not mean I want pleasure in this mo—" The argument dies on his tongue as I stroke the full extent of his throbbing manhood. His eyes shift behind me to Max and Leo's sleeping forms.

"As they've stated, they do not mind, and I quite enjoy this. Please allow me to ease your ache." I shift slowly down the bed and take him in my mouth, reveling in his widened eyes as his breath stutters.

"Powers Above, you're more magnificent than I have dreamed." He moans softly before his hands find my hair as he thrusts against the back of my throat. I feel a sense of pride as hushed sounds of his pleasure fill my night.

K ole is wrapped around me as I wake. The bed is otherwise empty, which strikes me as odd. Max and Leo hardly ever leave me to wake alone, especially given the current situation. The warm puffs of breath on my neck and strong arms encircling me serve as a reminder that I am, in fact, *not* alone.

I stretch, and he grumbles in his sleep, pulling me closer. The way I fit against him feels rather nice. His erection throbs against my backside, and I swallow hard, thinking about last night. Or maybe it was this morning?

I'm unsure of what came over me.

Something about the sadness and loneliness I see in Kole's eyes draws me to him. Even now, I feel comfortable wrapped up like this. Other men have never made me want a connection, aside from my husbands. But somehow, he's different in a way I can't quite explain.

Max and Leo insisted that they're okay with the concept of me pleasing him, and I acted accordingly. But perhaps I did too much, and they needed to step away? Prickles of worry travel up my spine as I lie here and wonder.

Before long, the door opens and Leo is there, face shrouded by shadows. I extract myself from the warmth of Kole's embrace and sit up in the bed, unintentionally waking him. As he yawns and rubs the sleep from his eyes, I see the moment he remembers where he is. A small jolt, a quick flash of panic crossing his face, as he looks to Leo.

"Good morning," Max calls from the hallway behind his brother.

Together, they enter the room with warm smiles, settling my nerves in an instant. Leo is carrying a previously unnoticed basket of bread, and Max is toting a tray piled up with eggs and vegetables.

"Oh! Breakfast in bed again?!" I clap my hands together, shimmying my shoulders. "This is a lot of food."

"Well, there are four of us to feed now, and it's our last meal here," Leo replies, gaze drifting to Kole. "I never did ask. You are aware of how to access the gate, correct?"

Still attempting to make himself small, he nods once, keeping his chin lowered.

"What seems to be the problem?" Leo hands me a piece of toasted bread and sits in a chair at the foot of the bed. "Are you having second thoughts?"

"Did you not enjoy yourself last night?" Max adds nonchalantly as he takes the seat next to Leo, placing the tray on the end of the mattress. "Surely Phoebe did not disappoint you, so tell us what the issue is."

Kole's eyes dart to the two of them, then to me, and he looks as though he may flee. "I apologize for not showing greater restraint." His hands are fisted tightly in his lap. "She was far from a disappointment." His words fade to a near whisper.

"Did she do the maneuver with her tongue?" Max asks, brow lifted as he takes a bite of melon.

"Maximus!" I gasp, shocked by his gall.

"What? It's rather enjoyable. Say what you will about marital training, but that little flick you do just at the tip." He sighs, fluttering his lashes with a drunken grin.

"Sh-she did. It is rather enjoyable." Kole's cheeks heat as the words leave his mouth. He continues to avoid eye contact with any of us.

"It is quite pleasurable, and the best part, Darling, is how much *you* enjoy doing it. I could listen to your moans forever. It took a lot of restraint last night to merely lie there and enjoy them."

"You were awake?!" Kole straightens in his seat, face draining of color. "I-I do not know what to say, how to properly apologize. Please do not punish her for my brazenness."

"There is nothing to say. Max and I have grown accustomed to sharing things. While it may have only been with one another, we are not opposed to sharing with you. So long as you are willing to share in return." He leans back in his chair, sipping his glass of juice.

"You said it yourself. You're one of us now, whether you like it or not. Judging by the manner in which your eyes consume her form, and how easily you fell into bed, I'd say you're happy to be here." Max flashes a bright smile at him.

"Forgive me for my disbelief, but this situation is peculiar to say the least." Kole takes a bite of his egg and hums. "That said, this is by far the best breakfast I've ever had. Thank you for your hospitality. You could have easily starved me and used me, then left me for dead. But instead you're just... including me. Making me food, allowing me to enjoy your wife's mouth." He bites his lip, dimples popping as he blushes.

"You may enjoy more than her mouth, so long as you're both in agreement," Leo states plainly, as though he's not turning Kole's world upside down.

"But men do not share their wives."

"We do," they confirm at once.

"If you do not wish to partake and love her as well, that is your decision. We merely ask that you respect her time and energy." Leo looks between us.

"Do her desires not matter?" Kole asks, causing flutters to come alive within me.

I offer him a tender smile and pass a look to my husbands.

Max beams a vibrant grin at him. "You see, the way you've taken her feelings into account speaks volumes about the type of man you are. Not to worry, Leo and I were abundantly aware of her attraction to you from previous run-ins. The instant she spoke to you in that soothingly sweet tone of hers, we knew she had already decided you're hers. Who are we to deny her?"

As Kole tilts his head to look at me, it is my turn to flush. "He speaks the truth, they have witnessed many of my emotions and have learned them well in the short time we've been married."

"So, if I want to try kissing, that would be acceptable? It appears to be rather enjoyable." He raises his eyebrows and looks around the room.

Nods from Max and Leo bolster his confidence. Slowly, his hand finds my chin, tipping my face toward him. My breath catches, eyes fluttering closed just as our lips touch. He's unsure of what to do at first, but when I press more firmly and open my mouth the smallest amount, he slides the tip of his tongue along my lower lip. I gently nibble in return, drawing a groan from deep within his chest. We continue with a slow, sensual push-and-pull, exploring one another. As we separate, his hand leaves my chin and promptly covers his lap.

"A natural reaction, I'm sure Phoebe would be offended if you didn't want to bed her after a kiss like that." Max chuckles, voice gravelly.

"I... why did we stop doing that?" He looks around the room.

"I'm not entirely sure. Nobody truly knows what happened during the collapse, but something drastic occurred, and New Promise was built by what remained of humanity, or so we are told. Generations have passed, so the truth is muddied at best." Leo pops a piece of fruit into his mouth.

"How peculiar. The Guides... well, they deny us any sort of intimacy as guards until we're proven worthy of procreating." He adjusts his hips, tucking his erection down. "I have never pleased myself nearly as well as you did, Phoebe. You're stunningly beautiful, and I may be inexperienced, but I know what attraction feels like. I could not stop myself from admiring you every time I was fortunate enough to be in your presence. Truth be told—" He blows out a trembling breath, jaw working as his face falls. "—you were my chosen bride. I am the reason the Guides tried to deny Leo the right to marry you."

I gasp, paling under the weight of his words, but say nothing and allow him to continue.

"Prime Guide decided that, since I had shown no recent interest in the available 'stock', he would offer Raymond a handsome reward if he reclaimed you." He swallows hard, hands fidgeting in his lap. "When Raymond did not return, he suggested we come and take you away by force. I wanted no part of it, and the instant I saw how you were thriving here, I decided I would die alone before separating you from Leo." Tears splatter on his plate of food, words hitting me full-force.

An eerie silence swallows the room. My breaths come out choppy and cold, not from anger, as I would have suspected, but from sadness and aching for him. I look to Leo and Max, who are understandably upset, but they give me the opportunity to make this choice.

Whether I decide to forgive Kole or not, they will stand by it.

"You wanted to marry me? This is why you watched so closely at our wedding? Why you've always given me inappropriate amounts of attention in public? I had thought they were tests, ways for the Guides to filter out the unsavory women. Have you truly been longing for me?"

Clearly in shock from my line of questioning, he startles and drags his sorrowful eyes up to meet mine. "Yes. I've always found you to be the most beautiful woman in New Promise. Your horrendous upbringing drove me mad with rage, and I wanted nothing more than to free you from it. Know that I never meant to deceive or hurt you. I simply required time to work up the courage to be honest. After last night, I felt even more compelled to come forward before anything more could transpire between us." His hand twitches, as if he's resisting the urge to reach for me.

"Your reasoning is fairly similar to that of Leo and Max. The three of you are very like-minded, and I can admire and appreciate your chivalry. Knowing Prime Guide Ogden, I believe that stealing me away was his idea alone. I do not fault you for any of this. You're a gentle man, I can see the compassion in your eyes." I extend my hand and take his.

He squeezes, firm but comforting, and looks to Max and Leo for a moment. Their jaws are clenched, but softness gleams in their returned gazes. "Surely this will not be easy, and I understand if I've ruined my chance at happiness here. But I would like to explore intimacy with you, Phoebe. With Max and Leo's blessing, of course, and I would like to do so without secrets eating me alive."

"I would like that. I never planned on having two men, let alone three. But some part of you speaks to a part of me. Your heart is pure, and I do not condemn you for wanting love. Just know, if you never feel love for me, that is fine. But the feelings I have in your presence are very similar to the ones I share with Max and Leo. That is why I'm willing to allow you the opportunity to try. I nearly squandered my chance at happiness with them by reacting poorly to their own secrets. I will not make that mistake again." I lean in and timidly kiss his cheek.

The tension in his body dissipates, and I glance at my husbands, their breathing is visibly more relaxed as they nod in unison.

"See, they may have been upset by your original confession, but they're not irrational, nor are they the type to lash out. There are few things that we cannot talk through."

"I thoroughly appreciate the understanding and the opportunity to be heard without harsh judgment. I've wanted to cherish you for so long, and I could not live with myself if I kept the truth concealed."

"That's admirable," Max says with a slight smile. "I will say that it upset me, but I understand that we didn't allow you the chance to bring it up before now. You're also not at fault for the Prime Guide's actions."

"I appreciate you for communicating and not wanting to start a relationship built on deceit. You're respectful, and that's what matters." Leo tips his head, and his face shifts to one of pure focus. "Now that we've cleared the air, we must prepare. I know we had planned to leave tomorrow, but with the Prime Guide not returning, surely the rest of the Guides are plotting to come find him. This is why we must leave before dawn." Leo stands and dusts himself off.

"It is not even dawn yet?" I ask, finally understanding why everything feels off today.

"No, Darling, we slept for a few hours, but must be on our way. Max and I finished loading the wagon already."

The air grows strangely cold in our room. Despite my excitement to escape this life, I'm just now processing the reality that this dwelling, one I've begun to feel at home in, will never be ours again. My lower lip juts out as I look at Max and Leo. Tears well in my eyes, and I inhale a trembling breath.

They move in unison—all three of them—to comfort me. Leo pulls me to his chest as Max comes up behind him and kisses me softly over his shoulder. Kole, despite his awkwardness, doesn't hesitate to rub my back in support.

"Darling, I know this has become our home. But wherever we settle beyond these walls will be so much more than this. So long as we're together."

"I love you, my steady Leonidas." I pull back and kiss him with conviction before turning back to

Max. "And I love you, my sweet Maximus." I softly bring my lips to his. "And Kole, we've only just become acquainted, but you're already special to me. I assure you that your life is in good hands with these two. Thank you for trusting them, despite everything." His gaze falls to my mouth, giving me the confirmation I need to kiss him as well. "I thought I was lucky to find one decent man, and now I've been blessed with three. You're right, Leo. Wherever we settle, we will make a home for ourselves."

"That's the spirit, Dearest." Max flashes a bright smile at me. 'Now, we really must be on our way."

We ascend the steps to the surface, and I sigh, taking one final look back down the hatch before closing it.

Leo grabs hold of the wagon handle and looks to Kole. "Lead the way." He tilts his head toward the hedge opening.

Kole is the first to step through the threshold. I follow close behind and leave Max and Leo to the wagon behind us. The world stands still when I take in the sight that awaits us.

"Finally, we were beginning to wonder if there had been an issue. It has been hours, Kole." The burly guard before us says, his gray hair immaculately trimmed.

At his flanks are two more, all past their prime, but imposing nonetheless.

"Why is she not in shackles? Where is the Prime Guide?" another guard—short and stocky—asks.

My eyes scan the surrounding area, searching for more of them. I find none, thankfully. There are three of them and four of us; I like the odds.

"Oh, he's dealing with Mr. Koeler. Not to worry," Kole tells them with a surprising amount of conviction, silencing the doubt in my mind.

He's not going to turn us in.

"Well, we're not to leave until he is ready. Please secure your future wife," the gray guard says, lip curling as he examines me.

"She is not a threat; she is here willingly." Kole places a hand on my shoulder, and I do my best to lean into him.

Where are Max and Leo?

"It was not a request, Kole. You know the rules as well as the rest of us. Until she's rightfully yours, she is to be contained." The short guard steps forward the slightest amount, and Kole stiffens. His grip on my shoulder tightens, jaw working as he tries to conceal his reaction.

Rustling behind us momentarily breaks the tension. Leo is the first to appear, the wagon just behind him, with Max hot on his heels. As they stop and look around, I see the calculation in their eyes as they exchange a look and nod.

"Gentlemen," Leo greets them, voice casual as he reaches back for his dagger.

"Gentlemen," Max repeats, smirking as his eyes harden.

Their preparedness and confidence make my blood run hot. When Kole braces himself before me, I nearly melt.

They're all ready for a fight, and I'm eager to watch.

"What is the meaning of this? Who are you?" the gray guard spits, eyes bouncing between my twins.

"Where is the Prime Guide?" the third asks, breaking his silence.

"Dead," Leo says plainly.

"I killed him, quite liked the feeling. You want to be next, or are you going to let us pass?" Max's voice leaves no room for doubt.

"Kole, what have you done?" the short man asks.

Instead of answering, Kole turns and slots his lips over mine. For just a moment, the looming trouble ceases to exist, and I drink him in. "Let us handle them, Precious," he whispers against my lips, eyes darting behind me with a silent order.

"Powers Above, you've been corrupted," one man says. I'm unsure which, because the next second, there is a flurry of movement.

A tussle breaks out, and I slip behind the wagon as I watch my men handle the guards.

Max springs into action, spearing the tallest guard—the quiet one—with his shoulder. His air escapes with a grunt as he slams into the ground. Max rears back and bludgeons him with his bare fists. The man wails as his nose makes an un-settling crunching noise and blood sprays every-where.

The gray guard bolts for Leo, attempting to take him down. By the clumsiness of his movements, it's clear that they have little combat training, and he's about to be sorry that Leo is the one he chose to pursue. In a smooth motion, Leo draws his blade. It gleams in the low morning light just before making contact with the man's throat. Precise as a surgeon, the cut slices a vital artery, and the guard grasps his neck, falling to his knees with shock alight in his eyes.

"Sorry, hazard of the job, I suppose," Leo leans down, wiping his blade clean on the man's tunic before sliding it back into its sheath.

Amid all the blood and chaos, the final guard comes for me. As he lunges, I reflexively sweep my leg out and knock him off-balance. Kole, having chased after him, manages to place the short man in a headlock, grunting as they struggle to overpower one another. My guard is larger, stronger, and in his prime. The poor fool stands no chance.

"This was supposed to be easy!" Max shouts as he wallops the man below him. "All you had to do was leave and let us pass."

"W-we cannot allow h-heathens to—" the man in Kole's grasp goes quiet as his trachea collapses, body falling limp.

"The only heathens in New Promise are the Guides and their lies," Kole spits, lip bloodied from where the man head-butted him during their struggle.

"Maximus," Leo says impatiently. "I know you're enjoying yourself, but we must be on our way."

His brother huffs in annoyance before landing a final, devastating blow against the man's battered face.

I rise from my cover behind the wagon and admire the chaos surrounding us.

What do we do now?

Chests heaving, my men move without a word. Together, they grab Max's victim and silently carry his body back beyond the hedge. I follow and watch as the three of them toss his corpse down the hatch, unceremoniously.

"Will anyone ever find them?" I don't know why I ask. But as they dispose of the second man, Leo's nearly decapitated foe, I can't help but wonder.

"So be it if they do. We will be long gone," Leo huffs out, just as they leave to gather the last body.

They return with the man Kole strangled and chuck his remains down into the depths of New Promise, with the secrets they all died for. I swallow, breathing in the relief, and turn to see hints of uncertainty on all three of my men's faces. It's clear they're worried, and my expression is not giving them the confirmation they had hoped for.

So I smile and stroll over to them.

"Thank you all for being my heroes." I kiss Leo first, wiping a smear of blood off his cheek.

"Anything for you," he mutters against my lips just as I pull away.

"My brave guard." I lay my palm against Kole's face and his eyes flutter shut. "I know you were never trained to deal with something so heavy, but your commitment to this, to us, is clear. Thank you for stepping up." I reach behind his neck and bring him down to meet me halfway. He lets a whimper slip free as his hands find my waist. Leo grips his shoulder, watching as we savor each other.

When we separate, his softened gaze and kiss-stung lips make my heart skip.

I turn to my third man, approaching slowly as his hungry eyes drink me in. "Are your fists okay?" I ask, taking his bloodied hands in mine.

He lets out a small laugh and smirks. "It's not my blood."

"You really let him have it." I give him an impish smile.

"One could say I pictured all the men who've ever wronged you... which is a lot." He leans into me, mouths a whisper apart. "Please let me taste your appreciation."

And I do, because I cherish him, all three of them.

He pulls me close, tongue slipping into my mouth, sense of urgency forgotten.

"Powers Above," Kole breathes out.

"I know," Leo groans. "As much as I enjoyed our post-murder tryst before, we really must make haste."

Max pulls away, chest heaving as he helps me steady myself. "My apologies, adrenaline is still in control."

I make a mental note to seek him out the next time he has any sort of rush. My cheeks flush at the thought of his intensity, the things he would do to my body.

"We should wash up before leaving, no?" Kole asks, taking in the blood on Leo's tunic.

"Where we're going, some blood is the least of my concern," he responds with a shrug.

"Very well, let's proceed." Max motions toward the opening, and we all follow Kole out.

Our wagon sits untouched amidst the blood pooled on the ground. Perhaps it will rain again soon and wash the evidence away; if not, we will be whispers on the wind before repercussions come knocking.

"Are your hands truly okay, or will Kole and I need to take care of wagon duties the whole way?" Leo asks Max.

"They're fine, a bit scuffed, but I know how to land a proper punch. His face was less solid than the bags I practice on." A faint chuckle escapes him, and Kole lets out a snort.

"I am glad I was on your side in that fight," he says. "The gate is this way."

We follow the perimeter wall for quite some time, keeping as quiet as possible. The only sounds disturbing the still morning are the scuffing of our shoes and the crackling of stones under the wagon wheels.

As we reach the back alley nearest the town hall, Kole guides us around a corner. It's dark and smells oddly musty, but the shape we find amid the haze is unmistakably a door.

"This is it?" Leo asks, voice filled with doubt.

"I know. They make it sound like an imposing thing, as if some enormous drawbridge lowers, sending you out into the wastes, but this is it. One metal door, one secret code, and you're on your own," Kole states, pressing the number pad. As it lights up, he pauses and looks at us, face illuminated by the glow of the screen. "I sure hope you're right about this. If not, it was lovely to experience a small bit of companion-ship."

Kole punches in the four-digit code, followed by a green light and a click. We collectively hold our breath as he slides the door open. I'm not sure what each of us was expecting, but surely it wasn't this.

Dry, cracked ground, barren hills glowing or-ange on the horizon under the light of the rising sun. No oasis, no vibrant tropical paradise... Nothing at all.

Leo blows out a harsh breath and lowers his head in momentary defeat.

Max comes to his side and slaps him on the shoulder. "We must travel for some time first. You've read the journals. Do not be disheartened this early on, we've yet to even step into this world."

"He speaks the truth," Kole agrees. "I've not read the journals, but surely New Promise has been strategically isolated to maintain their lies. We pick a direction and walk. Yeah?"

"North," Leo says on a sigh as he straightens. "The journals have mentioned heading south to get back. So, we go north now." He nods his head in the direction and holds a device I hadn't noticed before.

A compass.

Together, the four of us take our first steps out of New Promise and into our new lives.

Clicking noises echo on the wind, signaling the locks engaging behind us. The mechanical whirring seals our fate. I turn and look, shocked to find the exterior keypad destroyed.

There really is no going back.

Not that I'd want to.

Even as I peer at the dimly glowing horizon, I feel a strange sense of hope flood my system. The dry earth beneath our feet should feel ominous, but I trust Leo's research. He's been reading and notating, sleeplessly plotting our route for the past week.

"If we stay true north, we should reach a small oasis in about a day's time. Then a settlement rests a short distance beyond that. We have more than enough rations to last until then. Let's get a move on," Leo looks back at the three of us and nods, confidence returned.

"From November on," I say with a loving smile.

"From November on," he and Max repeat.

Kole looks between us, brows pinched, and mumbles, "From... November on?"

Max turns to him and grins. "That's our mantra. From November on, our lives are ours to live. Happy, healthy, together. No silly laws, no Guides. Nothing but our love for one another."

"I like it." Kole flashes a dimple-framed grin at us, the first I've seen from him, and repeats, "From November on."

My stomach feels a familiar flipping sensation from his excitement. Hours ago, he nearly devastated me, and yet I cannot deny the way I feel for him.

"Wonderful. Now, we must get a move on." Leo takes hold of the wagon handle and leads the way, compass in hand.

Foolish daydreams made me imagine a lush paradise on the other side of the barrier walls. While that is not our current situation, I still maintain a smile. Leo surely feels responsible for all of our survival, and I need to keep a brave face for him.

Truthfully, I had expected this scenario, so I'm not entirely caught off guard.

We watch the sunrise together, something we have been denied as a community due to the stone walls surrounding the entirety of New Promise.

As the warm glow lights the valley, I gasp. It may be dried up, with nothing more than a few dead trees scattered about, but the sight is wondrous. Max pulls me to his side and kisses my cheek as we stop and admire the scene.

For a few breaths, we watch the morning sky as the reds and oranges fade, washed away by a vibrant blue. Kole takes my hand in his, face glowing under the sunlight. As he turns to me, I tug on his hand slightly. Immediately understanding my request, he leans down and gently claims my lips.

"You have freckles," I whisper as he pulls back. "I hadn't noticed in the dim light." His face pinches, eyes falling to the ground. "Do you not like them?" I ask and place my palm against his cheek.

"They are a flaw. Neither of my parents possesses the trait, so I do not know where they come from. My red hair and these 'dirty' marks are anomalies in the community. Others have not been kind in regard to them." His jaw tightens.

"I think they're stunning. You're unique, and I find you *very* attractive."

"You like peculiar men, Phoebe." He laughs through his nose, looking me in the eye. "You're beautiful inside and out. Never stop being you."

I step up onto my toes and kiss him with more intent than before.

Leo places his hand on the small of my back as I pull away, tenderly pressing his lips to my cheek. "She is spectacular. I'm glad you understand how special she is and why we fought for her. I'd love for us to indulge right this moment, but we've barely made any progress and must return to our travels."

I have never known daylight to be so bright. The reality of our sheltered existence hits me with force. All the generations stuck inside those walls. "Do you truly believe that the Guides know we're not alone?" The words fall from my lips as they cross my mind.

"I know they do." Kole's statement stops all of us in our tracks.

"What do you mean by that?" Leo raises a brow.

Kole swallows hard, attention volleying between our faces. "I have... heard things. Being assigned to guard Prime Guide Ogden granted me entrance to some interesting meetings."

"But you had only been a guard for three months," Max interjects.

"I was only his *personal* guard for three months. I have been a guard to the Guides for two years, since I turned twenty-one, and had only recently been deemed seasoned enough for the *prestigious honor* of guarding the unofficial king of New Promise." Spiteful and bitter, his words drip with disdain. "The way he controlled everything—every citizen—was repulsive. He knew there was a life outside of New Promise. He had the keypad outside destroyed the last time someone returned, to ensure no more 'rescue' attempts were made.

The Guides live in luxury, while the people of New Promise are indoctrinated from birth. It's compliance built on fear and ignorance."

"Then what of you?" Leo steps toward him. "Did you intentionally let him die so you could escape?"

With a tight expression, he nods. "New Promise will be in equally horrid hands without him, but you were the ticket to my freedom. I had not expected that you were planning to leave as well. Please understand that I would never betray the three of you as I did that deplorable man. I merely played ignorant until I felt safe sharing my knowledge." Tears form in his eyes as his voice wavers. "Strange as it may seem, you're the closest thing to a family I've ever truly known, even if it has only been hours. I feel like I belong here."

"So this is why you accepted our offer so easily, and never put up a fight?" Max steps to him alongside Leo. Their shoulders squared and rigid.

"I understand your anger, truly. Please understand my reasoning. I'm not a monster, merely a man who yearns for more than the bleak future New Promise offers." He shrinks further under their scrutiny.

It's a sight to behold. Such a large man buckling under their judgment.

I clear my throat, and the three of them turn to face me. "Leo, you murdered my father, did you not?" I place my hands firmly on my hips.

Kole goes still as Leo's shoulders sag, and he nods. "Indeed, I did."

"And you had your reasons for that, correct?"

"To protect you! He was going to take you back, and surely you'd have suffered at his hand," he argues back.

"And you, Max, was it not your hands that took the life of the Prime Guide?"

"Yes, but it was also to protect you, Dearest." He lowers his gaze to the dusty ground.

"So, help me understand how Kole is in the wrong for not interfering? Should he have fought when you released him? What would you have preferred? He aided you in taking out those three guards, did he not?" Silently, I wait as they look between one another.

Kole keeps himself still, eyes closed as he awaits their answers. As if watching them work it out would physically hurt him.

Leo watches him for a short while and finally speaks, "I suppose you did not act any differently than I would have in your situation, given your knowledge and shared opinions on the way things are governed. And your help was appreciated."

"He speaks the truth. I only ask that you never keep things like this from us again, unless we part ways. But while we're a group, honesty is paramount. You've shown us twice now that you don't want to live with the ghosts of your choices. But please, if there are any other secrets, speak them now." Max folds his arms and waits.

Shocking us all, Kole wraps his arms around both of them and sighs while they embrace each other.

"There is nothing else. I truly do not enjoy keeping things from those I care about. I also would like to stay by your sides, even after we find a place to settle. I, well, have had a wonderful time with the three of you." Cheeks flushed, he pulls back and looks between them, then over to me.

"I am not the one who needs convincing." I snap my gaze to Leo and Max. "Are the two of you comfortable with him staying?"

"We are." They nod.

"Wonderful, can't have my men at odds with one another." A coy smile tugs at my lips.

Panic, shock, and finally realization take over Kole's face before Max claps him on the shoulder. "Seems as though you're stuck with us, Freckles."

"You are one of three people allowed to call me that," he grumbles with a faint smirk.

"Now that we've settled our first lovers' quarrel, we must be on the move." Leo tips his head and starts walking.

We follow him blindly into the dusty expanse.

We've been traveling for quite some time. My feet ache, and the dust is clinging to every sweaty inch of my exposed skin. Everything around us is still desolate and barren. I'm doing my best to maintain high spirits, but this is a test of my will, which, thankfully, is stronger than most. Never would I have thought that growing up in an abusive household would be a hidden blessing. No matter how harsh our reality gets, I've endured far worse for nothing.

Max is pulling the wagon now; they've rotated between the three of them several times. We've stopped for a quick break to eat some rations and hydrate, but otherwise have stayed true to the plan.

Leaving at this time of year seems to have been a great idea, as if we had any other option. Still, the sun has brought warmth, but it is not overbearing. The lack of shade could prove treacherous in any other instance.

Nightfall is near, and we will soon need to locate a place to camp. One last looming hill and Leo has sworn we can stop. Kole pushes the back of the wagon as Max and Leo pull at the handle. Slowly, we crest the top, and I drop to my knees when I see the salvation before me.

Green and lush, a small oasis tucked securely in this valley. Our first sign of life beyond the wastes.

Tears streak my dust-covered face as my men whoop at my side. Fresh adrenaline courses through my veins, and I make a wobbly sprint to the crystal-clear pool of water.

"This is it! This oasis is connected to a small river, which is great news," Leo cheers from behind me.

Kicking off my shoes, I step into the cool water and sigh.

"We shall set the tent up, and then I can find our soaps and clean tunics, and we can bathe," Leo announces.

"Bathing sounds like the perfect reward for a hard day's work." I sigh. "I cannot wait. The water is spectacular. Slightly cool and crystalline."

We quickly raise the tent, securing it to the nearest tree, just in case the ground anchors fail. Leo quickly lays out fresh tunics and finds some soap he tucked away in the wagon.

"This is why you were left in charge of packing the essentials. I never would have thought to bring soap to the wasteland." Max nudges him playfully.

"You never can be too prepared." Leo shrugs, sorting through his bath supplies.

"Well, I will be in the water if any of you require my attention." I shrug out of my tunic and leave it where it pools on the ground, strolling leisurely toward the water.

"Powers Above," Kole breathes out behind me.

"She is a vision, dressed in the glow of the setting sun," Max says in response.

"You two can stand here and watch all you like. I'm joining our wife," Leo announces.

I step into the spring and turn just in time to witness the twins disrobing. Even covered in dirt and grime, the sight of their nude forms makes my heart rate increase. Leo holds a bottle and a sponge as he approaches, a knowing smirk on his face. Max is right behind him, sporting a heated expression.

I peer over his shoulder and find Kole off to the side of the water, still in his filthy tunic. His face is flushed bright red, hands fidgeting at his sides.

"Are you not going to join us?" I ask, sure to keep my voice soft.

"You would want me in that way? Even after my secrecy?" He does his best to keep his gaze on my face as I wade through the water to him.

"Did we not reach a mutual understanding?" I tug at the string securing the top of his tunic, trailing my fingers between his sizable pectoral muscles. "You must have had a rigorous training routine." My hand lands at his waist, resting over the tie there. "May I?"

His swollen manhood jumps below the fabric as he nods. His attention shifts behind me to Max and Leo, intently observing while lazily palming their erections. Kole swallows hard as I undo the knot, and his tunic falls free.

"Are you uncomfortable with this situation?" I ask, voice hushed. "If so, we can figure out an arrangement that will work."

"No." He looks to me and shakes his head. "I-I've never... I don't know how to do any of this. I do not want to disappoint you."

"You'll only disappoint her by not trying. She's easy to please. We will show you how," Leo affirms behind me.

"But not until we all get cleaned up. So please make haste." Max chuckles.

I take Kole by the hand and lead him toward the water.

Leo immediately goes to work lathering the sponge. As he drags it across my body, Max trails his hands through the suds and scrubs away the grime. Kole stands just behind them, lips slightly parted. Focused intently, his eyes follow the way Max moves his fingers along the contour of my breasts and hips.

As I tilt my head back, Leo pours soap into my hair and looks to Kole, silently ordering him to step in. He shakes his head, blinking away his entrancement and goes to work, kneading my scalp. I moan under their attention, aching in ways never before known to me.

Once I'm thoroughly cleaned, it's my chance to return the favor. Standing in the waist-deep water, I can't help but admire their erections bobbing gently on the surface. I bite my lower lip in an attempt to contain my arousal as they watch me with matching fires in their eyes.

I'll likely need another scrub down by the time this night is over.

oving toward my men, I feel empowered by their hungry gazes. The thought of three is slightly intimidating, but I've grown accustomed to my twins, so adding another handsome man into the mix is doable, surely.

Taking the soap and sponge from Leo, I begin with him, drizzling the clear liquid over his bare chest. I start with my hands, trailing slowly down his torso, watching his nostrils flare as I grip his manhood and stroke. Just as he closes his eyes, moving his hips, I stop and switch to the sponge. He groans as I tease, but sighs when I begin lathering him up.

Max, eager to get to the real fun, takes the soap from me and pours it on himself, handing it to Kole, who does the same. A small laugh bubbles out of me as I finish scrubbing Leo. He turns me around, wrapping me in his arms. Slowly, I drag the sponge over Max, biting my lip as the water streams over his bulky chest.

"You're going to drive me mad, Dearest." He leans in and kisses me, thrusting into my hand as I take hold of him.

Kole lets a faint moan slip out, and I pull away from Max, turning my head to him. He acts on impulse, stepping to our side to claim my lips for himself. Leo kneads my breasts, nipping at my shoulder as he slips his hardness between my thighs, moving in a slow, steady motion.

Max's warm mouth finds my neck, nibbling at the sensitive skin in the way he knows drives me wild.

As Leo thrusts forward, granting my clit much-needed attention, I moan and toss my head back. Max and Kole pull away, panting before me, and exchange a look that I cannot read.

But Leo understands.

Tangling his fingers in Kole's curls, he forces him to turn his way. "Do it, Pretty Boy. You both want it." I swallow hard as he releases his hold.

"Come on, Freckles, I won't bite... too hard," Max says with an impish smirk as Kole shifts his focus to him.

Leo presses forward again, drawing a whine from my throat as the tip of his hardness nudges my entrance. I nearly crumble as Max and Kole's lips meet. My body burns as I take hold of both of their erections, gripping and working as their tongues dance together.

"Spectacular, Darling, let me feel your desire," Leo growls in my ear as his hand slips around to circle my clit and slides me onto his throbbing length. He teases me for a moment, slowly working in and out as we watch the show Max and Kole are putting on. Their hips move, helping me work them, and Leo increases his pace. Before long, he's groaning in my ear, holding me upright as my knees fail.

A few deep thrusts paired with his deliberate strokes, and my pleasure boils over. I scream with my release, and all three of their hungry mouths return to my pebbled skin, nibbling and sucking as they pant against me.

They continue leisurely enjoying the waves of my release while the fire in my veins dwindles. Leo, still impossibly hard, eventually scoops me into his arms. Max and Kole follow closely behind as we proceed toward the tent.

"That was an easy one. I think we can break the record tonight, boys." Leo chuckles with a devilish edge. He lays me out on the surprisingly plush makeshift mattress, propping my head up on a few pillows. Kneeling next to me, he strokes himself and looks at Kole. "You first, Pretty Boy. It's about time you experience the luxury of our wife."

Max steps behind Kole, trailing his hand over his shoulders and down his arms. "Don't worry, we'll show you exactly how she likes it. I can't wait to watch you please her." He kisses him just behind the ear.

Kole swallows hard, kneeling between my thighs. "You're divine," he says, eyes traveling over my entire body. His large, warm hands rest on my hips as he settles in, hard and dripping with pre-release. He slides himself through my wetness and shudders, resting just at my entrance. Gliding his fingertips along my shins, he stares down in disbelief, throbbing against me.

For a moment, I question whether he'll ever push forward, until Max takes his manhood in hand.

"You're nearly as large as I am. She'll squeeze you wonderfully." Kole groans as he strokes him from the tip, straight down to his thick base. "Please don't keep us waiting. I want to watch your face flush as you experience her perfection."

Sinking slowly, one delicious inch at a time, his eyes nearly roll to the back of his head as he fills me. Max moves to my side, and I take hold of him, stroking slowly. Leo brushes a knuckle down my cheek, and I turn to take him in my mouth.

Kole, with a strangled moan, finally centers himself enough to open his eyes. Some part of him comes to life as he watches me with the twins. His first thrusts are shallow, but effectively nudge an extremely sensitive spot inside me. I moan around Leo and he pulls back to let me breathe, brushing my hair from my face. I take him in my hand and smile, moaning louder as Kole drives into me harder, steadier.

"Guide's mercy, you're warm—" He shudders. "—so very warm." Hissing as he pulls back, the blazing desire on his face as he watches himself re-enter me is erotic. "Powers Above." He tosses his head back, increasing the pace of his movements.

Max silences my mewls with his manhood, taking my throat for his own pleasure.

I'm so lost in the sensations that I hardly notice Leo stepping away. He kneels behind Kole, who goes still, seated deep inside me. "You're doing so well, to think that you were nervous," Leo murmurs, lips a hair's breadth from Kole's ear. "You're a natural. Shall we bring her to the peak together?" I watch as he places his hand on Kole's back and leans him forward.

Max pulls out of my throat, giving me the opportunity to kiss Kole. As I nibble softly on his lip, he gasps, hips jerking slightly. I peer over his shoulder and observe as Leo slowly presses a finger into his back entrance.

"My brother is a big fan of anal," Max says with a chuckle, running his fingers through Kole's hair.

"Something he reads about in the old books he enjoys."

"I am," Leo confirms, "though I usually fill Phoebe's back entrance as Max claims her front. This would be quite an experience." He slips another finger into Kole and I'm given a front-row seat as his eyes light with pleasure. "Shall I continue? Or would you like me to stop? One more finger and you'll be ready to take me, Pretty Boy."

"P-please," Kole whimpers against my lips, needy and eager.

"Please, what?"

Time stands still as we await his answer. Max lazily strokes himself, and I trail my fingers lightly up Kole's muscular arms. He bites his lower lip and lets out a shuddering breath. "Please claim me, Leo. Let me feel you in ways I never knew I needed until this very moment."

With a sharp inhale, Leo gets to work preparing Kole. I lay my palm against his cheek and look into his eyes as he grunts from the third finger working inside him. "It feels amazing, you'll see. Leo is a very generous lover and will show you pleasure like nothing you've ever known." I kiss him and devour his sounds of ecstasy while Leo presses the tip of himself inside.

Slowly, Leo pushes further, working Kole deeper into me in the same breath. I whine and arch my back as they move with shallow thrusts. Kole finally shifts, taking the last of Leo's length with a garbled groan. Max moans at the sight, and I nearly erupt, whimpering as I throb around Kole.

"Our wife has a need." Max takes hold of Kole's hand and guides it down between us, finding my aching clit. "Just like this, I understand you're likely overwhelmed, but Leo will thrust for you." He guides his fingers, showing him exactly how I like to be touched. I work Max with my hand as I writhe below them.

Leo growls, pressing harder into Kole. "Perfection, you're everything we needed to make us whole." Leo's movement drives him into me and sends me promptly over the edge.

As I scream, tightening around him, Kole becomes frenzied. Groaning and trembling, he leans forward, taking Max in his mouth.

Max hisses, thrusting and clenching his jaw, showing Kole no mercy.

I continue to ride out the intense, unyielding waves of pleasure as they drive one another to the brink of release. Leo slams into Kole repeatedly, skin clapping together in the night. Max holds tight to Kole's hair, muttering incoherent praise as the motions force him deep into his throat. My core tightens once more, throbbing in search of release.

"Please," I beg to no one in particular. One hard thrust from Leo pushes Kole to hit the perfect spot, and I tremble as I come undone.

"That's three," Leo moans as I claw at Kole's back, crying out their names.

"Kole, I need to feel her," Max says, pulling free from his mouth. I'm nearly boneless, limp against his chest as he pulls me off Kole. "You're doing so well, Dearest." He kisses my forehead before maneuvering me onto my knees. "Go on and take care of Kole, I've got you." He slides slowly into me from behind, moaning my name as my walls pulse.

"He won't last much longer," Leo leans back, situating Kole in his lap. As I look up into those blissed-out blue eyes, I smile and swirl my tongue around the tip of his manhood. When I have him in my mouth, Max thrusts into me and I let out a muffled moan, choking as Leo pushes him deeper into my throat. I'm impossibly full, being driven to tears from the sensations. They work in perfect rhythm, driving into us just right. The second Kole is almost out of my mouth, they rock us back together and drive him into my throat.

"That's it, Darling, take them both. Show Kole exactly how amazing you are. Such a good wife." Leo thrusts harder, faster. "You handle me so well, Kole, Guide's mercy. The way you let me use you for her pleasure is divine." He continues, rhythm increasingly frantic as his release grows near.

Max increases his pace behind me, position changing slightly. Leaning forward, he slams Kole's mouth to his, swallowing the sounds he makes, and Leo erupts, hips jerking with his release.

The sensations cause a chain reaction. Seconds later, hot streams hit the back of my throat, sending my system into a frenzy. I press myself back into Max, meeting him thrust for thrust as I throb around him, breaking apart once more.

He leans us back, pulling me against his chest. "Let me taste him, Dearest." As our mouths meet, he groans, tongue slipping between my lips. Deeply seated inside me, he shudders, and I feel a familiar rush of warmth. As he rides out the last of his climax, his hand finds my clit, coaxing a final orgasm from my oversensitive body.

"Wow," a breathless Kole says, half asleep with Leo still nestled inside him. "This—" he moans as Leo kisses the side of his neck. "—has been the best thing I've ever experienced."

I offer a half-conscious smile to him. "You're ours now."

"She speaks the truth. I'm pleased to hear this was to your liking." Leo shifts, finally slipping free. "I quite enjoyed pleasing her while pleasing you. It was something I thought I'd only ever get the chance to read about." He takes Kole's jaw in his hand, eyes dancing across his face before kissing him. "Thank you for being perfect for us."

"I have never felt so adored." Eyes glistening, Kole winces as he moves to sit beside me.

"It's only tender for a little while. You get used to it." I lean over and kiss him, still in Max's lap.

"We should probably go and clean up." Max wraps his arms around me and rests his chin on my shoulder as I feel him slip out of me.

"Good idea, Brother." Leo stands, coming to help me to my feet. He pulls me against him and embraces me, looking deeply into my eyes. "I love you, Darling. Thank you for trusting me. We broke our three-orgasm record." He laughs softly.

"You've only ever been good to me, of course I trust you. I love you dearly... The orgasms are a bonus." I flash a sleepy smile at him.

His face lights up, and he lifts me into his arms, placing a kiss against my forehead. "Let's get cleaned up and get some rest. As long as we follow this river, we should find a city tomorrow."

After we quickly rinse ourselves, we fall into the soft fabric of our traveling bed, and I sigh. Leo comes to one side, Kole to the other, with Max wrapped around him. We waste no time getting settled.

Tonight is the beginning of something beautiful.

The men surrounding me are all I truly need, but a community where we're accepted and allowed to exist without fear of banishment would be amazing.

Hopefully, tomorrow will be the day that becomes a reality.

Today is going quite well. I woke up with a hint of worry, unsure of what my men would think after last night's developments. Fortunately, it seems they've grown closer. I'm glad to see that Kole has adjusted so quickly and fallen into place with ease. He fills a void that none of us knew existed.

I look at him and see a man I *chose*. Not that I love the twins any less; they're phenomenal, caring, and loyal. I would never replace them. But Kole speaks to me on a different level, and I can't deny the magnetic pull I feel for him.

Clearly, the twins feel it as well, and I look forward to *many* repeats of last night.

We have been walking since before dawn. The sun is now high overhead, and Leo is confident we're nearly there.

Wherever "there" is.

Another large hill awaits us, and we immediately go to work pushing the wagon up to the top. Our bodies are sore and exhausted, but we resist the urge to quit, urging one another on until we crest the seemingly infinite hilltop.

We gasp in unison at the settlement nestled in the valley on the other side. I nearly tumble as we cheer loudly.

Paradise, that is the best word I can use to describe the utopia before us. It appears to be at least twice the size of New Promise, only there are no walls, no uniform, identical dwellings. These are *homes*. Each is a colorful representation of its inhabitants.

Fence-lined fields sit off to the sides where cattle are grazing. I know we had a few in New Promise, mostly for the Guide's butter and cheese production, but there are dozens, maybe hundreds, scattering the landscape here.

"It's real." Kole's eyes glimmer as we speed-walk toward the haven.

"Great work on navigation, Leo," Max praises, grinning from ear to ear.

Abundant grass and flowers cover the ground, except for a strangely sculpted walkway.

"This is man-made," Leo explains. "Trails were carved into the terrain to aid people in their travels."

We fall in line on the smoothed path and proceed toward our future.

A group of citizens—about one hundred, if I were to guess—gathers near the entrance as we approach. What catches my attention first are the women. They're smiling and wearing *pants*. In fact, not a single person that I can see is wearing a tunic. Not one wife is cowering behind her husband. Children are frolicking in a small park just beyond the threshold, and I see at least three different types of dogs scurrying about.

"Greetings," Leo calls out as we grow close enough to hear. "We, well, we are here seeking sanctuary, should you be willing to take us in. If it would be too much of a burden, we only ask for a place to sleep for the evening, and we shall move along to find a different home."

"Are you more cultists?" A large man breaks through the crowd. His clothing is far nicer than anything I've ever seen, even beyond the luxury tunics the Guides wear. Warm brown hair swept back, and he has a rather impressive beard.

"Cultists?" Leo rears his head back.

"Religious extremists." The man scans our tunics with his eyes. "You look like the ones who come from that place. Are you refugees, or zealots?" He folds his arms as the crowd grows larger.

"W-we're—"

"Boys?!" Leo's words are cut off by a man's bewildered voice. "Margie, oh my. Marge, it's our boys."

Through the crowd, a familiar, deep-skinned older man comes into view. Max takes my hand and squeezes, choking on a sob as Leo wobbles next to me.

"Leonidas? Maximus? You're alive? You're *here*?" The woman next to him gasps, hands covering her chest. "My babies!" Her pale skin and graying blonde hair are unmistakable.

The twins are frozen in place until Kole nudges Max.

"You—" The previously denied sob bubbles out of him as he drags me toward the crowd, Leo just behind us.

Our audience watches with tear-filled eyes as my husbands embrace their long-lost parents. Silence falls, and they weep together for some time. Sniffles muffled by shirts, they share an embrace for the ages.

"We thought you were dead," Leo mumbles into their father's shoulder, eyes red and glossy.

"We've been here all this time. We attempted to return for you, but the code to the gate had been changed."

"The entire control panel is destroyed now," Kole informs him.

"And who might your friends be, boys?" Their mother asks through the flurry of emotions. Wiping away her tears as she smooths her hair and tries to appear dignified.

I see which parent the twins inherited their proper mannerisms from.

"Mother, Father, this gorgeous, wonderful woman is our wife." Leo wraps his arm around me, kissing the top of my head as he struggles to regain his composure.

"Sweet Phoebe Harding, I'd recognize you anywhere. That hair and those eyes, just like your mother. Though the last time I saw you, you were but a young girl. Raymond had already started displacing his anger on you." Their father smiles softly at me, a familiar smile of powerless pity. "Such a horrid life you suffered through. I do hope my boys are treating you with the love you deserve." His deep brown eyes, just like the twins', shine brightly.

"They are, Sir." I nod with a soft smile, unsure of how to properly address him. This is not customary, my husband's father would never acknowledge me if we were in New Promise.

"Please, it's Father, or Arden if you'd rather." He pulls me into a warm embrace, and now it is my turn to sob. A lifetime of pain eased by one simple act, a mindless one for him, but it means everything to me.

Acceptance.

Relief.

Peace.

"And who might you be? You're a dashing young man." Margie looks at Kole with a raised brow.

"Kole Barton, Madam. I'm... well." He chews his lip, looking between the twins and me.

"He's our fourth," Max confirms, pulling him in for a chaste kiss on the cheek. "*Our* boyfriend."

Kole's lower lip quivers, and his eyes soften, filling with tears. I recognize his disbelief and hopeful trepidation. Tension in his shoulders betrayed by the sparkle in his eyes.

"Sweet boy, come here." Margie pulls Kole against her, rubbing his back as he sobs into her shoulder. "Welcome home, you're family now, too. Anyone special to our little miracles is special to us."

Max joins in their embrace, and we all share watery, heartfelt looks.

"Well, I suppose since you're Koelers, you have references and can stay. Welcome to Utopia Springs. I'm Merrick, the unofficial mayor." He laughs. "We don't truly have a hierarchy here, everyone just does their part to help us thrive as a village. Though I run the protection force, three strong young men such as yourselves would be great assets. Ever put out a fire before?" He raises his brows.

"I'm sure we can learn, we're quick studies," Leo responds with a nod, voice rough from the emotional overload. Still, he manages to present himself as professionally as possible.

"Oh, but of course, the sons of historians, surely you were some of the most informed members of that wretched place. No wonder you got out and could find us. Come now, we'll sort out an empty house that the four of you can occupy." He tilts his head toward the heart of the village.

As we follow, I observe all the vibrancy and uplifting colors surrounding us. Nothing could have fully prepared me for how alive the world is. Not only are there animals and plants, but the sky itself seems somehow brighter.

"We're constantly building and expanding to make room for our growing community." Merrick looks lovingly at a woman sporting a very swollen belly. "From what I've heard, thanks to your parents, there are some freedoms you'll have now that did not exist in New Promise." He steps up to the front of a two-story home. The outer walls are painted a sunny shade of yellow, appropriate for the brightness that I feel just from being here. "First, you may decorate your homes however you please. This one is quite large, there should be room for at least a few children, should you choose to have them."

"Ch-children?" I swallow. "We... we can have *children*? At will? Multiple?" Questions, nearly incoherently, fly from my mouth.

"Ah, yes. There are no foolish laws to prevent you from doing so. We also do not ration our food. Every person here contributes in some way and understands that indulgence is frowned upon. But we do not impose limitations. Your neighbors, however, may judge you if you're greedy."

"We cannot have children," Kole says, voice filled with contempt.

"We can remove the sterilizers, should you prefer. Our doctors are also versed in the removal of that horrid poison capsule," Merrick states, and I watch all three of my men's faces fill with hope.

"Would you be interested in gracing us with a child in the future, Darling?" Leo takes my hand, eyes shining with silent desperation. His words may not say it, but his expression yearns for it.

"I would love to," I reply with a bright smile, and it is the truth. In New Promise, I would have loathed the thought of bearing a child, but here? Seeing the little ones frolicking about freely, giggling as they chase one another. I want that future for my babies. One I would have thought impossible.

"Wonderful. We adore children around here. There are a few schoolrooms to teach them skills based on their aptitude and interests. I shall leave you to explore. I would highly recommend that you stop at the tailor's shop." Merrick nods and leaves us to settle in.

The crowd that followed us here disperses with him, and we're left standing on the front step of our new home. Margie and Arden are all that remains of the group that had gathered, faces still light and filled with a combination of joy and disbelief.

"Well, Lovelies, shall we unload your goods? I'm eager to catch up with my boys and get to know my new son and daughter." Margie says, looking toward the wagon.

We step inside, and the first thing I notice—aside from the fact that it's fully furnished—is the lights. I spin around in the center of our large main room and admire the brightness, how clearly I can see everything.

"She's precious." Arden chuckles. "Electricity is commonplace here. We draw ample power from the river nearby. You'll all have plenty of things to adapt to, and there will be some community-based experiences that will shock you."

"Society has advanced rapidly outside of New Promise. Not being crippled by false prophets has done the rest of the world wonders. We have horses and trade routes with nearby villages as well. The collapse seems to have erased the worst of humanity, aside from New Promise. The protection force exists to keep people safe from environmental factors," Margie explains, placing rations in the large, cooled storage box.

"Merrick called it a cult," Max says, placing a stack of books on a shelf near the plush brown sofa.

"Because it is, Maxie. Surely it began as a haven after the collapse, but through generations of willful ignorance and fear-mongering, they've kept the Guides in power, while silently banishing all who oppose them. They're abundantly aware that New Promise is not the only village in the world, but spreading that knowledge means they lose their following and with it, their status," she says with a roll of her eyes. "I suppose, for them, it's better to be the king of nothing than to be another 'commoner' in a thriving world."

"I'm just elated to see you alive and well," Leo speaks up. "Years of mourning your loss, while trying to maintain our secrets, have been trying. I'm infinitely grateful that it was not in vain. My only regret is that it took so long." His voice cracks and he sighs.

"Likewise. We were going mad not knowing your fate. Our hopes shattered when that door didn't unlock." Arden sighs, face dropping into a sorrowful grimace.

"I just want to interrupt and thank you for your acceptance of me," Kole says to the countertop, shying away from our gazes.

"Dear boy," Arden says, voice warm, as he steps toward him. "We do not merely *accept* you. If you make my boys happy, that is all I need to know. The same as Phoebe, you're family." He wraps him in a crushing embrace, and Kole lets free the tears he's been struggling to withhold.

A warm, genuine smile pulls at my lips. It's on course to become a permanent fixture at this point.

"You love all of them?" Margie asks, stepping to my side as Leo and Max join the huddle with their father and Kole.

"I do. Truthfully. Kole has just come into the picture, but it feels like he's always belonged with us." I sigh, fighting my emotions.

"My boys have always been lovers at their very cores. I knew they'd find the perfect partner. I never would have guessed they'd find two." She pats me on the shoulder.

"What exactly are the jobs like here?" I ask, directing my focus away from the overwhelming amount of love filling me.

"Not to worry, the boys will be fantastic on the protection force. Their main duties will be patrolling to ensure nobody needs assistance," she answers.

"I was not referring to them." I swallow and turn to face her as the men carry on a conversation of their own.

"Oh, Dear, what do you enjoy? I know my boys must have shown you many hobbies."

"I was quite fond of the hens and tending to the garden. I would see to both of their care each morning after Max and I made breakfast."

"Oh! That's wonderful news!" She claps her hands together. "I manage the western farm. You could accompany me and see how you like it. We have cattle, hens, swine, and a few trade horses to care for. There is also a garden there, though the main one is on the eastern side of town."

"I think I would enjoy farming quite a lot."

"Amazing! We'll go by tomorrow. I can introduce you to our herds. For now, I say we make some dinner. I'll pop over to our house and grab some ingredients. Keep our guy's company for me." She plants a motherly kiss on my cheek and slips out the door.

I sit and listen to the men talk about training for the protection force, excited to be part of a team instead of being forced into isolation. As Margie returns, Max and I fall into a comfortable state of normalcy, preparing food. I chop herbs while he sautes a variety of vegetables I could never have imagined. Casual conversation fills our space as if we've been doing this forever.

As we gather around our brand-new dining table, love surrounds us. My face grows pained from the persistent pull of my grin.

We made it.

EPILOGUE

4 YEARS LATER

Few things in life will ever compare to moments like this. Leo is lying curled in a ball with his favorite person. I'm not bothered in the slightest that the title is no longer mine. From my seat in the chair next to our bed, I smile, admiring how much Harriet looks like the twins. Even at three weeks old, it's obvious one of them is her father—they don't care which. She's a welcome new addition, much anticipated after Kole fathered Samuel.

Max enters the room, tray in hand, and smiles at the sight. "Dearest, I brought you some tea and a breakfast sandwich. Would you like to eat here, or move to the balcony?"

"You had better have enough for all of us," Leo grumbles from the bed, shushing Harriet as she stirs. "I'll put her in her cradle, and we can enjoy a nice breakfast together," he whispers, shifting carefully.

As he rises to his feet, he delicately scoops our daughter up, laying a soft kiss against her deep black hair.

"I'll go find Kole, meet us at the table, my lovely wife." He kisses my temple and glides out of the room.

We have fallen into place beautifully over the past four years. My men are heroes in the community, having saved several lives. It is amazing how many people attempt to swim in the river with no practice or knowledge beforehand. Fires are also more common than one would think, but nothing unmanageable.

Margie and I tend to the farms together, and I've bonded quite strongly with the cattle. Such beautiful, gentle giants.

I sit at the table, smiling brightly at Kole as he drags his feet with Samuel on his hip.

"Rough night?" I ask as he strolls my way with his little red-haired clone.

"I cannot wait until he's done with this teething business so I can rejoin the three of you. But my boy needs comfort, and my Precious needs rest, so sacrifices must be made." He yawns.

"Hey now, we rotate nights." Max chuckles as he enters the room.

"I know, but it's as if he *knows* I'm the reason he exists, and punishes me more harshly for it," he grumbles.

"Well, let's hope our princess is not as vindictive in a few months." Leo beams as he finds a seat at the table.

"I can't believe he was fine for the first few months, and now, almost two years old, he's decided teething is too much." Kole sighs, eyes half open as our son sleeps in his lap.

"Do we need to take the day off from our duties for you, Love?" Max asks, passing him a pitiful look.

"You're running yourself ragged, Handsome. Max and I will gladly tend to the children while you and Phoebe catch up on some much-needed rest," Leo offers.

"Oh, I can't miss my first day back at the farm," I argue.

Kole whines, face pulling into a pout as his eyes fill with desperation.

I bite my lips and shake my head. Of course I'm going to give in. "Fortunately, my boss likes me," I concede and giggle as he silently celebrates to avoid waking Samuel.

"Well, you've given her two perfect grandbabies, so she'd better," Max jokes and kisses my cheek.

Soft laughs echo through the room as we enjoy our breakfast, as we do every morning, be it at the table or in bed. Our time here has been the definition of perfect. Utopia Springs has surpassed even my most unrealistic dreams. To think this wonderful place was so close all along.

On occasion, I think of New Promise—the people still living there, how they all deserve to know a life like this. Margie assures me it's a healthy thing to contemplate, but not to worry about. The people there know no different, and some of them are exactly where they belong.

As selfish as it may seem, I know she's right. We couldn't go back if we wanted to anyway.

And I don't.

I have everything I love right here.

Keep up with Rii

Hi there! If you've made it this far, I must have done something right! If you want to stay up-to-date on my current and future projects. **R iiFinley.com** has all my relevant links!

Thanks for reading!

Acknowledgements

Wow, this book was a journey. I couldn't have done it without a few awesome people!

John, as always, Thank you for listening to me ramble out the idea for this novel at 2am. Even if you have no idea what it's about, your willingness to let me babble on for hours about a world I was literally making up on the fly was so helpful.

Tenny, Tenneth, TenTen. I want to thank you for spearheading the writing challenge that sparked the idea for this, and for your continued hype through the entire process.

Ancy, because I'll forever refer to Leo as "Horny History Man" and that's on you.

Lexi, Duh, Of course you were THE hype for months while I wanted to cry over the mess this started out as. Everyone needs someone like you in their life.

About the Author

R ii Finley is a coffee-drinking, music-loving introvert. She finds joy in all kinds of creative outlets from painting and sculpting to writing (obviously). She loves animals and has two rambunctious boxer dogs. The Spotify team is probably concerned by how much of her listening time is consumed by Sleep Token.

Romance novels are her escape—her happy place—she's usually reading one on her phone in her down time.

If you love good banter and lighthearted humor in the midst of chaos, and prefer your books spicy and heartfelt with a splash of darkness, you've found your new favorite author!